MIND YOUR MANORS

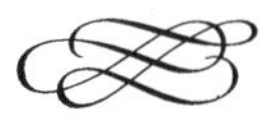

CEECEE JAMES

For my flock of flamingos

CONTENTS

BLURB

Mind your Manors

by CeeCee James

The story began with ex FBI agent Oscar O'Neil (and his dog Peanut/Bear) from from the Baker Street Mysteries. This series is written from the point of view of his granddaughter! Will she learn the secrets of why her grandfather is estranged?

Meet Stella O'Neil. She's got a lot on her plate, trying to figure out her crazy, stubborn family and starting out as a realtor. Throw in a dead body found in what used to be the town's "royalty" family's manor, and she's neck deep in a mystery.

She may be sweet, but she's pretty stubborn herself.

As Stella's curiosity leads her from one town resident to the next, a dramatic tale of family secrets starts to appear, but is she getting too close to the truth? A scary car chase in the dark has her nerves on edge, but she won't give up until she finds out who the skeleton once was. She's so close... but someone... maybe more than one person... will do anything to stop her.

CHAPTER 1

Fireflies flashed around in the cool night. I didn't move, hoping one would land near me. It had been a long time since I'd seen the tiny warriors of light. Twenty years, maybe.

I guess I was about five or six when we'd moved away, Dad and I. Mom was out of the picture, and had been for a while. I hardly remembered anything about her. Dad didn't like to talk about her, and I didn't ask much. Growing up, life had seemed normal having it be just Dad and me.

We moved all the way to Washington state because Dad needed a fresh start, and he sure got one. I'd loved living there. The ocean, the mountains, city life, it had it all.

Now, I guess it was my turn for a fresh start, and so I'd

returned to my childhood stomping grounds of Brookfield, Pennsylvania.

The porch swing squeaked under me as I absentmindedly brushed off a mosquito. I closed my eyes and breathed in, sipping on the memories of my childhood.

Summers in Pennsylvania should be on everyone's bucket list. Although it was cool, now that the sun had slipped below the horizon, the warm scent of blackberries still hung in the air. I rocked and stared up at the sky. The overhead branches from the maple tree blotted out most of the stars. But on a clear night, if I were to start down that path that curved into the backyard, the night sky would make me gasp.

Growing up in Seattle, I'd never known how brilliant and clustered the stars really were. The city lights had drowned out a lot of the night sky.

Of course, logically I'd known there were billions. I'd even done my sixth grade science project on the birth of stars, with my father watching over my shoulder as I carefully spread the glitter.

"Stella," he'd said. "More up here. You can't just clump them all in one spot."

Well, it turns out, stars can be clumped in one spot. Like right there. Staring up gave me the weirdest sensation. Like I could fly off the earth and spin among them. I pulled my gaze down to the earth, to the little stars—the fireflies—before me. These I could handle.

Remembering that day of the science project gave me a strange feeling, too. My dad was pretty straitlaced. Come to think of it, I'd rarely seen him smile. There was that one time when his stock meeting had gone well. And that time he brought home a BMW. He'd sat six-year-old me in the passenger seat and talked about how this car was one of the best ones ever made.

"Stella, you put your mind to it, and you can own one of these some day."

I'd sat straight on the white leather seat, my light-up sandals not quite reaching the floor, and stared at the wood on the dash. It had gleamed with an iridescent quality to it, something I might now compare to a tiger's eye. But, back then, I just knew that it looked alive. The fire in the grain called to me. I'd slowly reached out a finger to touch it.

"Stella." His tone warned me to not smudge the interior.

It wasn't that my dad was mean. In fact, he rarely raised his voice and never spanked me. He just had a way about him. I couldn't put my finger on it. He was a typical type A personality, while my own personality was probably somewhere near the end of the alphabet.

Still, we were all each other had. He never even dated again, saying he wanted to focus on raising me and getting his company going. That I was enough.

I tried to live to be enough for him. I wanted to make him happy and proud of me. I was always on the honor roll, gymnastics, the science team. I'd graduated college magna cum laude, and then been offered an executive job with Costco corporate.

My personal dating life hadn't been so great, though. I think I needed to figure out more about men, about my dad, my mom and the rest of the family. Maybe I just needed to figure out my own complicated noodle brain.

So, I ended up leaving that job, and here I was sitting outside of my rental house across the country, the signature on the rental contract practically still wet from signing it that morning.

The quiet was something new and would take time to get used to. The hustle and bustle of the city had seemed almost like family. I held my breath to listen. A breeze moved the leaves above me, making them say shhh shhh, as if they were wishing the world sweet sleep.

My dad had been unhappy that I'd moved back. "Why Pennsylvania, Stella? Why are you leaving a good job? This isn't using wisdom." He'd then gone into his typical detailed list of what consequences I could suffer with future retirement issues.

I'd tried to explain to him that Uncle Chris had offered me a job. Uncle Chris was Dad's younger and more adventurous brother. He was kind of a playboy but hadn't had a serious relationship in years. He owned a real estate brokerage out here in Brookfield, Pennsylvania, and I had heard rumors he was thinking about getting into politics. One night last Christmas I'd had one glass of wine too many and somehow my whole disillusionment with corporate America had spilled out. Uncle Chris had listened with a twinkle in his eye, and then told me he could give me a new beginning with a new adventure.

"You're too young to feel like this. What are you? Twenty-six? Seven? Come work for me. You'll love it. The real estate market is hopping, and every day there's something new. You need a life, girl. Heck, when are you going to meet a man?"

Well, a man was the last thing I wanted. But the idea of an escape sure was tempting. So, when Uncle Chris had called me a few months ago to remind me of his offer, I'd jumped on it.

But an escape wasn't the real reason I'd moved out to Brookfield. I could have done that anywhere.

I moved back here for my grandfather.

Oh, he didn't know I was back. I wasn't sure what he was going to say when he saw me. In fact, growing up, I'd thought he was quite an evil man from the stories my father had told me. But I had too many mysteries revolving around family, and I needed some answers.

It was time to find out for myself.

CHAPTER 2

Tuesday morning found me inside the realty, ready to hear my first assignment. Unfortunately, I had to wear the same clothes I'd had on while driving across the country. The delivery company had promised it would be here yesterday, but they hadn't shown. A bored woman informed me over the phone that there'd been a severe storm and the truck was stuck in a washout. "Just a few more days, ma'am. If you can be patient."

My rental had a washing machine but no dryer, so here I was, in clothing that hadn't quite dried from the night before. The dampness was lovely. I sat in Uncle Chris's office and tried not to squirm.

"So when's the moving van getting here?" Uncle Chris took a sip from a coffee mug that said *World's Best Boss*. He leaned back in the chair, and it squeaked in protest at his considerable bulk. For the last twenty minutes, we'd beaten to death every small topic two people who barely knew each other but were still family could tackle.

Sunlight vainly fought through the dirty window to brighten the room. A filing cabinet—half the drawers unable to close from the overflow of papers—was a pedestal for a drooping plant. Brown leaves littered the floor. And the craziest thing, pink flamingos decorated everything. They were on his desk, on the window sill, and one giant flamingo poster competed with pictures of himself with his arms around different blonde-haired bikini girls.

I swallowed hard, wondering what I'd gotten myself into.

"Stella?" Uncle Chris prompted.

Oh, yes. He'd asked a question. "Hopefully in the next couple of—"

"Nice," he interrupted. "Ah! Here she is now."

The door creaked open behind me. I turned as a slim woman with short blonde hair and a skirt covered in a kaleidoscope of flowers entered the room.

The woman was as animated as her outfit. She blurted in a rush, "You can't believe traffic. It was insane!" She ran to the desk in a swirl of perfume and threw down a packet of papers. "Anyway. Tada! There it is."

Uncle Chris pulled over the folder and flipped it open to read. He announced without looking up, "Kari, this is my niece, Stella. She'll be assisting you until she gets licensed."

Kari's blue eyes took me in. Smiling, she held out her hand. "Kari Missler. Nice to meet you."

I shook it. "Nice to meet you, as well. Have you worked here long?"

"Oh, I'm fairly new myself," she answered.

"She's still under a probationary period," Uncle Chris grumbled, flipping another page.

Kari's cheeks pinked and she laughed. "So far so good, though. I hear you're from Seattle?"

"Yeah, but I was born in Pittsburgh."

"Should have stayed here, as well," Uncle Chris added. "That father of yours..."

My dad had always been somewhat on the outs with Uncle Chris. All the men in my life were so complicated. Was it any wonder that I had dating problems? I was thankful for the job offer, but it did make me wonder if Uncle Chris was competing with my dad somehow in trying to be a substitute dad. Or maybe my uncle thought having family working in the business would be good for his image. Like I said, he wanted to get into politics.

"Oh," Kari smiled. "So there's some family dynamics at play here, huh?" She shook her head and whispered conspiratorially. "Don't worry. I get dynamics like that. You're going to do great."

Uncle Chris slid the packet of papers over. "You forgot to have them sign here." He tapped the empty spot with a finger. "And there's two spots where a set of initials are missing."

Kari's mouth dropped open. "Oh," she said, blankly. Then smiling brightly, she accepted the papers. "I'll get right on that. In fact, I'll pop over there, now."

"Take Stella with you," Uncle Chris said. "Have her help you with the staging."

"You got it," Kari said with a nod. Then, turning to me, "You ready?"

A few minutes later, we climbed into what appeared to be an innocuous van. I was expecting a sedate drive when Kari hammered on the gas, and I was thrown back, violently reminded that appearances can be deceiving. She took the last corner with tires screeching, and me hyperventilating and stomping the floor like I was praying for a brake pedal.

I think I was.

She pulled into the driveway of an old Victorian manor with a calm smile. I, on the other hand, breathlessly clutched my seatbelt.

Kari didn't seem to notice. "Okay, so let me catch you up to speed. This is an unusual seller." She peered at the house over the tops of her sunglasses. "Two retired sisters and a brother. All in their late seventies and early eighties." She grabbed her purse and the folder of papers. "Staging is going to be tough, I'm afraid. The house hasn't been aired out in eons. Fortunately, with all the land and the historical value, the property is worth well over a million dollars. I'm expecting we'll get a nice chunk of cheese at the end of it." She opened the van door and climbed out.

I struggled with my seatbelt which had locked tight during one of her turns. Her eyes were down scanning the forms when I finally joined her.

"Don't let them intimidate you, especially the older sister. Her bark is worse than her bite. There's a brother around here. I haven't met him yet, but I hear he's a prankster."

I studied the enormous manor and swallowed at her comment about the sister.

I scanned the yard as we walked up to the door. Dry bristles of grass struggled through the brick pathway. In fact, it seemed all the landscaping plants were gasping for water.

My toe caught the edge of an uneven brick and I lurched forward.

Kari grabbed my arm. "You all right?"

I nodded, embarrassed. We walked up the stairs where Kari opened the screen door. She knocked while I continued to study the architecture. The porch was long and curved around the side of the house.

"A veranda," Kari murmured, catching my glance. "Very nice description to put in the listing. Always talk it up."

A tall thin woman, wearing a brown tweed dress, answered the door. She leaned on her cane, her lips frowning with disapproval.

When I say thin, I mean skeletal. Her other bony hand clung to the door as if she were about to slam it shut in our faces.

"You again," she said. Her voice could make a puppy whimper.

"Hi, Ms. Valentine. I'm sorry, but there was a spot I missed having you sign. And since I was coming over, I figured I'd bring my assistant. She'll be helping you get things ready."

Here Kari touched my elbow. "This is Stella O'Neil."

Ms. Valentine stared down her nose that jutted between sunken cheeks. "Not even wearing a business suit. How charming," she said dryly.

I brushed my t-shirt down over my jeans. "I'm new in the area. Unfortunately, my moving truck got delayed. Anyway, it's nice to meet you." I thrust my hand out toward her.

She glanced at it before taking it with a surprisingly firm grip. I swear, she squeezed just to be mean.

"Well, I suppose you must come in again." Ms. Valentine stepped away from the door. Her cane thumps echoed as she walked down the huge hall.

We followed her into a room that I assumed was a study. The windows were streaked with grime, and clutter was everywhere. I glanced at Kari, wondering exactly what she expected me to do with this mess. I wasn't a miracle worker.

Ms. Valentine brought out an antique pen and raised her eyebrows expectantly at us.

Kari jumped. "Oh yes." She quickly went through the folder and pulled out the document, then directed Ms. Valentine where to sign and initial.

Ms. Valentine's stubbed pen scratched across the paper. Her signature was beautiful calligraphy.

"Okay!" Kari said brightly when Ms. Valentine had finished.

"Well, now. I'm going to leave you in the very capable hands of Stella O'Neil here. She'll need to get familiar with the house to begin the staging process."

My mouth dropped open. She wasn't abandoning me here, was she?

"Excuse us," I said to Ms. Valentine with what I hoped passed for a smile and then drew Kari outside to the hall. "You can't be serious. How am I to get home?"

She jingled a set of keys. "You can take the van home. It's the company vehicle anyway." She pulled out her phone. "My Joe is here." Then, sensing how nervous I was, she patted my arm. "You've got this. Nothing like jumping into the deep end of the pool to learn to swim. Relax, you'll be fine. I'll send you the number of a cleaning company to call, and this will all be done in two shakes of a lamb's tail."

I didn't appreciate the cutsie encouragement, and that sentiment must have shown on my face.

Rather than be offended, Kari laughed. "You've got to start somewhere, and right now you're on the bottom."

Before I knew what was happening, she was out the door and hurrying to a waiting car.

"But Kari!" I yelled.

She showed me no sympathy. Just waved and sped off.

Slowly, I turned back to find Ms. Valentine watching me with a sour expression on her face.

"Well, are you coming in or were you born in a barn? We don't normally keep the doors open in these parts," she snapped before walking away.

Feeling like a kicked puppy, I headed back inside.

Once in the hall, I heard a patter of little feet. The sound was jarring, and I glanced around for a child. To my surprise, coming around the corner was a woman who was scarcely taller than your average fifth grader. She exuded an innocent jubilance as her tiny feet danced across the worn floorboards.

"Hello! Hello!" she exclaimed, her hands clapping together. "Gladys! You didn't tell me we had guests."

Ms. Valentine turned stiffly and dipped her chin in my direction. "Sister, it seems the realty company has mistaken us for a babysitter. Starla is her name."

"Stella," I corrected and held out my hand. It was quickly grasped in the shorter woman's plump hands.

"Oh, how do you do? Isn't this so exciting!" she flushed and brushed a curl of her gray hair behind her ear. "Valentine Manor hasn't seen so much action in years." Her forehead puckered as she thought. "Not since the snowfall of '98. Remember that, Gladys? The mailman got stranded here!"

The much taller Ms. Valentine rested her hand on her sister's shoulder, the two sisters appearing like a lodgepole pine tree next to a squatty cabin. "Starla, this is my younger sister, also Ms. Valentine."

This time, I didn't bother to correct the wrong name.

"Oh, you can call me Charity. But, please. I don't need any more reminders that I never found a beau." She giggled. "It's never too late!"

"It's too late, sister," Ms. Valentine said with an assertive nod.

"You never know!" Charity defended herself with a pout. "It's not over until the fat lady sings. Or so they say."

Ms. Valentine raised a thin eyebrow. "I seem to remember you singing during your bath the other day."

Charity's mouth dropped. "Oh! That's unkind. That's so very unkind of you, Gladys."

Ms. Valentine ignored her and motioned to me. "I suppose you need a tour? Let's get on with it."

The first room was the formal living room. A stone fireplace, large enough to hold an enormous log, took up nearly one wall. As we stood admiring it, a crash came from the room to the left. I jumped and spun around.

Neither of the Valentine sisters reacted.

"Shouldn't we check to see if someone fell and is hurt?" I asked.

Ms. Valentine leaned against her cane. "There's no one here but us. You must realize, this house is very old. It will make an odd sound every now and then."

Charity giggled again. "Maybe we are bugging the ghosts."

I raised my eyebrows. Definitely not the answer I wanted to hear.

"So, why are you selling the manor now?" I asked, to change the subject. Casually, I walked around an old sofa, reaching to feel the thick tapestry covering. I immediately recoiled at the layer of dust.

"That's none of your concern," Ms. Valentine answered.

Okay. I tried again. "Will you be selling the furniture with the house?"

"Perhaps. If the price is right." She led us briskly from the room. "The company mentioned they would be hiring house cleaners. I don't trust them."

"We got rid of our last housekeeper five years ago," Charity said sadly.

"Might I remind you of our missing silverware?" Ms.

Valentine responded. "If we kept her we'd be down to our last spoon."

"We'll make it as painless as possible. Just a light dusting and a bit of a yard clean up," I hurried to reassure her.

In my head I was screaming, *Liar. Liar. Pants on fire.* It was going to take a heck of a lot more than a light dusting.

She took me through two more rooms and then we ended at a staircase. I pointed to the stairs. "Where do those go to?"

"This house has four floors. The upper level is completely closed off. We've taken to living in the three bottom rooms down here."

It didn't seem like she was offering to take the tour upstairs. That was okay. I figured I could check it out when the cleaning company was here.

Back at the front door, I assured the ladies I'd be back in the morning to help stage, and thanked them for their time.

As I walked out to the van, I called the cleaning company that Kari had texted to me. I made the appointment for the following day and then got in the van and strapped on the seatbelt.

Deep breathe. This could be done. Just need some rubber gloves and some glass cleaner. A whole lotta glass cleaner.

Feeling better, I put the gear in reverse and turned to look over my shoulder.

A huge man stood behind my vehicle.

I screamed and slammed on the brakes.

He lurched over to my door. I flinched, not sure if I should unroll the window or just get the heck out of there.

He had on a plaid shirt and jeans and appeared comfortable here. I vaguely remembered Kari mentioning there was a brother. I opted for the window.

"Hello, can I help you?" I asked.

"Did I scare you?" He stared with pig-eyes and showed no emotion.

"Ah, yes, you sure did." I nervously smiled.

There was no response other than a deep exhale.

My nerves crawled. "Was there something you needed?" I asked again.

"I like scaring people," he answered.

Well, now. The only thing that kept me from flooring the gas and getting the heck out of Dodge was the man's age. He appeared to be in his late seventies. Still, his hands looked strong.

"Okay, I'm going to go now," I said, slowly winding up the window.

"I'm Richard." He stuck his hand through the partial opening.

I licked my lip, staring at it, before timidly giving it a little shake. "How do you do. Very nice to meet you. Well, don't worry. I'm going to do a great job getting this house sold."

This elicited the first real emotional response from him. He frowned, his brows beetling together as he turned to stare up at the house. "My sisters are glad to be rid of it," he said. "But you can't always get rid of ghosts that easily. They have a way of following you."

Oh...kay. I was definitely ready to go. "I'll see you later, Mr. Valentine."

He backed away slowly. I noticed his boots were worn and mud-caked.

I reversed out of the driveway as fast as was politely possible. Once on the road, I chanced a quick glance in the rearview mirror.

He stood at the end of the driveway staring after me, his arms hanging by his sides.

And then he smiled. It wasn't a good one.

CHAPTER 3

The morning started with a gurgle. A literal one. I'm not sure what happened, but a wet popping noise in the bathroom—of which terrified me more than any nightmare—reluctantly dragged from my sleep and into the room to see what had happened. I peeked between my fingers. Sure enough, the toilet was overflowing.

I have no idea what happened. I had to squelch across the floor and locate the little handle behind the toilet to turn off the water. Which brought me up close and personal to more than I wanted to see... ever.

After throwing down towels the previous renters had left behind in the linen closet and calling Mrs. Crawford the landlord (who, with properly horrified tones, assured me she'd have a plumber right out) I rinsed off as best as I could and got dressed. It was time for me to leave my mess and clean up someone else's.

I had just pulled out onto the highway when my phone rang. My car's blue tooth sent the phone call through its speakers.

I clicked the green phone toggle on the steering wheel and answered, "Hello, Stella speaking."

"Stella. It's Dad. I haven't heard from you lately."

"Hi, Dad! Everything's going great here. I just got unpacked and I'm heading out to my first job. How are you?"

"Well, now. I was calling to see if you'd worked this so-called adventure out of your system yet and were ready to come home. I was able to wrangle an awesome job opportunity for you, but it's not going to be available forever."

Oh, he was trying to tempt me. Visions of the overflowing toilet, my bills and the lack of money spun in my mind. Not to mention the moving van still hadn't shown up. Then there was my task at hand with preparing the Valentine estate, with the boxes, and the dust, and the cold looks and creepy stares of the elderly siblings.

Back in Seattle, it's true, I had everything I could have ever wanted. But I was out here to push myself. To learn something. Dad, God love him, thought there was only one way to do things. And if I caved, I'd just be validating his belief.

I shook my head and said, "No, everything is going great here."

"That's not what your uncle says."

"You've been talking with Uncle Chris?"

"Of course, I have. I want to know that everything is going okay with you. And he says you had a disaster in your house this morning."

I frowned. How on earth could Uncle Chris have known about the toilet? Then I remembered that Mrs. Crawford was a friend of his. But why would she call to tell him about the bathroom incident?

"Everything is fine. Just a plugged toilet. Easy fix," I said breezily, trying to wash the swirling brown truth from my mind.

"You're stubborn, just like your mom," Dad said.

His words cut like a knife to my heart. I took a deep breath. But, not knowing the woman, I didn't know how to respond. Like usual. I felt a mixture of denying I was like her, and disloyalty that I was not defending her.

"Well, you always said not to be a push-over," I answered finally.

He snorted. "At least leave that grandfather of yours alone. He's dangerous. You have no idea who you're messing with."

"I haven't said anything to him, Dad," I answered.

"I moved you out to Washington to protect you. I can't tell you how frustrating it is to watch you go waltzing right back into the fire, with no regard or respect for what I say."

"I do respect you, Dad." I puffed my cheeks to hold back a sigh. I'd heard those words before. They were his old standby in every lecture I'd ever gotten.

"You need to listen to me, for once in your life."

"I hear you." I hit my blinker and took the exit. At the bottom, I turned left and headed into the town of Brookfield.

He exhaled deeply. "It's because I love you, Sweet Pea. That's why I warn you and bug you."

"I know, Dad. I love you too."

We said our goodbyes and then I hung up. How much more could happen today? My emotions were feeling tattered along the edges. I squeezed the steering wheel. *Okay, girl. Time to get my game face on. I'm in charge here. I'm going to be the best darn house stager Flamingo realty has ever seen. I'm going to—*

A blaring horn caused me to scream and swerve. A car had shot out of a blind driveway.

"Not my fault, you crazy—" I shook my fist in the rearview mirror at the retreating vehicle.

"Okay, Stella. Get a grip," I muttered to myself.

I pulled down the Valentine's long driveway. My insides felt weak and wimpy. Luckily, the cleaning service was already there. I parked next to the green-and-white van and got out.

A gal climbed out of the driver's side of the van.

"Hello!" she said, smiling brightly. She looked like a quintessential housekeeper, with a bandanna holding back her hair and a white uniform on. "I'm Denise. I guess we're doing a bit of house cleaning today, hmm?"

I immediately felt fortified seeing her. "That's right! I'm Stella, by the way." I turned toward the house and straightened my shoulders. "Okay, you ready to tackle the beast?"

She'd been pulling out a plastic bucket filled with cleaning supplies from the back of the van when I said that. She paused and asked, uncertainly, "The beast?"

I smiled, not knowing whether I was describing the house or Ms. Valentine. "Let's go," I said, and marched to the front door.

It opened as I climbed the squeaking stairs. Richard hung on to the doorknob with a ham-sized hand and stared dully at me.

I could hardly believe this man was a prankster. He looked more like a serial killer.

"Richard," I said, with more confidence than I felt. "We haven't formally met, but I'm from Flamingo Realty. Like I was telling you yesterday, we're here to help get your place ready for the open house."

"You going to try to get rid of the ghosts?" He stared with those tiny eyes. I glanced next to me. Denise was nowhere to be found. I turned and saw her reluctantly waiting on the bottom step.

Okay, then. Let's get this job over with. "I'm not sure about that, but we'll get it ready for sale."

There was no movement, not even a flicker of an eyebrow to show he'd heard me. Nerves tickled up my spine.

"Out of the way, Richard," Ms. Valentine came to the door and nudged her brother away with her cane. He moved heavily as though his boots were made of concrete.

"You're late," Ms. Valentine's bony hand gripped the iron head of her cane.

Late? I resisted the urge to look at my watch. I knew I wasn't late. I'm sure I'd mentioned I'd be here sometime this morning.

"Oh, I'm sorry," Denise rambled next to me, Ms. Valentine's accusation clearly had taken her off guard. She shifted her bucket in her hand. "I was told to be here by ten and so—"

Ms. Valentine ignored Denise like she was a fruit fly, and continued to stare at me. "You stated that you'd be here in the morning. I consider morning to be seven. Eight at the latest. We don't sleep away our lives here."

I'm just going to by-pass that little comment. "So," I said, with a million-watt smile. "We're here now and we'd like to get started so we can quickly get out of your hair."

"What a deplorable statement," Ms. Valentine sniffed. She stepped away from the doorway and we walked inside.

The house curtains remained closed and the interior was as dark as a tomb. I could hear Denise swallow as she walked next to me, the cleaner bottles softly clanking in her bucket. Ms. Valentine led us into the drawing room where Denise's eyebrows flickered as if she were tallying up what needed to be done. They quickly smoothed down. I was impressed with the job she did keeping her face emotionless. It *was* overwhelming.

"Oh, more guests!" Charity tottered around the corner. Her hair hung in old-fashioned little girl curls which bobbed as she turned to smile at all of us. "Sister, should I get the pie?"

"Not now. Go back up to your room and practice your piano."

Charity's grin fell. "But—"

Ms. Valentine ignored her. "Ms. O'Neil, if I could have a word with you."

"Of course." I followed Ms. Valentine out in the hall, momentarily taken back when I saw Richard standing by the drawing room doorway. It took everything to control the shiver as I passed him.

Ms. Valentine walked quickly. Despite her age and cane, her long legs made it difficult for me to keep up without appearing like a puppy chasing after its owner. She turned the corner into the study. Unfortunately, I had to catch up.

As soon as I entered, she began, "Ms. O'Neil, that woman is not to have free rein in my house. I haven't vetted her. I don't know who she is. We have valuables here."

That woman? Oh, Denise. And yet you left her alone to tell me. "I understand. However, she's with a very reputable company. We wouldn't have hired her if she didn't come highly recommended."

"Regardless, you will monitor her movements in this house."

"Absolutely."

"Very well," she waved her hand. Once again, I felt like that puppy, now being shooed away.

When I returned to the drawing room, Denise had disappeared.

Richard was standing in there with his hands clutched in loose fists. Just as I was about to ask him where she went, I heard the spitting of gravel from the driveway. I ran to the porch to see the green-and-white van leave in a cloud of dust.

What in the world had happened? Had he said something to her?

Quickly, I pulled out my phone and dialed. As soon as she answered, I blurted, "Denise, come back. I need you. Listen, I'll have you just do the kitchen. I'll make him leave."

"Sorry, Ms. O'Neil. I've heard too many things about that place. I'm not coming back. Not with that guy staring at me, telling me that my skin looked soft. I left the bucket of cleaning supplies on the porch. You can drop them off at the headquarters when you're finished. Or just keep them."

What things had she heard? I closed my eyes and said goodbye. Sighing, I slid my phone into my pocket.

Well, I *did* say I wanted an adventure. I wasn't giving up now. I rolled my sleeves, grabbed the handle of the bucket, and went back inside.

The first room I tackled was the kitchen. As I glanced around, I shrugged off the expectation of getting it clean and went with a quick "it's good enough" mop-down. I sprayed the counters and cupboard door fronts and wiped. Then I cleaned the sink and appliance fronts. The floor was going to have to wait.

After that, I walked into the drawing room and did a similar dusting with a lemon wood cleaner. I fluffed the pillows and beat at the couch with a rag. It was actually not too bad when I was finished.

It was the upstairs that was going to be the battle.

I dragged the lemony cloth along the wood banister as I walked up the stairs. In reality, I knew I couldn't do much. But I'd make sure there were no nasty surprises hidden in any of the rooms.

The thought of nasty surprises distracted me and I missed a step, catching myself with the banister. It really was a grand staircase. I could imagine how it was back in the day. Music playing as guests walked in. A butler at the door to take the expensive jackets. The laughter as the chandelier cast shadows of women in fancy dresses and men in top hats.

And then, I thought I could hear laughter, high and tinkling. And music playing... what in the world?

I froze at the top of the stairs and checked behind me. Just as quickly as I heard it, the music faded away. I held my breath to listen, but it was gone.

There had to be a reason. Maybe Charity. Yes! That was it! Didn't Ms. Valentine tell her to go play the piano?

Okay, there's no more time for imaginative fancies. Let's just get in and take a look.

The hallway was equally as grand with the walls hung with family portraits. I stopped at one, obviously the original Mr. and Mrs. Valentine. The man wore a full beard and smiled good-naturedly. His wife smiled too, a Mona Lisa one, like she was trying to hold back a laugh and be proper. Her little hand rested on top of his big one in a loving way.

The next one showed the same couple, this time each with a little girl. One seemed younger than the other and sat on her father's knee, while the older one stood next to her mother with her hands resting on the arm of a chair.

I recognized Ms. Valentine in the face of the older child. Even at that age, her lips were pursed and eyes stared straight ahead. Charity's head tipped to the side as she smiled.

The third picture showed three children, this time a sullen boy next to his father. Boy, did Mr. Valentine appear proud. He stood behind the boy with his chest puffed out and his hand resting on his son's shoulder.

And that was it. That's where the family pictures ended.

The doors lined the hallway, appearing impressive with their wooden embellishments. One by one, I opened them and peeked inside. White-shrouded ghosts in the shape of beds and dressers filled the rooms. I didn't clean much because there was nothing in the way that would stop a potential buyer from being able to walk through the room safely.

At the end of the hall was a stairway that reminded me that Ms. Valentine said the third floor was for the servants. There was also an attic, but no one could possibly expect me to explore that, could they?

I walked to the last bedroom door just before the stairs. There was a surprise waiting inside.

It wasn't a bedroom like the rest, but an old playroom. The walls were painted a light green color and two window seats were covered in inviting pillows. There was a rocking horse in the corner. Its wooden saddle had raw splotches from the peeling paint, but I could see it had once been bright red with gold trim.

In the middle of the room was a table with a chessboard on it. I walked over to the game. The pieces were still laid out as though the children had just run outside in the middle of playing.

There was a low bookshelf filled with children's books. One book lay open on the floor. Over against the wall was another shelf, this one neatly filled with a few stuffed animals and a doll.

Oddly, nothing was shrouded in sheets. A thick layer of dust covered everything instead.

At the far end of the room was a door. It caught my eye because it was narrow and plain white, so different from the others. The handle was made of cut glass, like a prism.

I walked over and gave it a turn. The knob was cool in my hand, but the door didn't open.

I twisted it harder and yanked with a grunt. It shifted as if it could open but was jammed for some reason. *Okay, last chance.* I yanked harder, half afraid I was about to break something.

It opened with a rusty squeal. A swirl of dust and cold air entered the room.

I peered in to see it was the entrance to a narrow staircase. Correction, a very narrow, steep staircase. I puzzled for a second before realizing it must lead up to the nannies quarters. I fished out my phone and set it to flashlight. There was no banister, so I reached for the wall for balance, its surface rough and unfinished, and headed up the stairs.

The first step squeaked under my feet, making me wonder if this was such a good idea. How long had it been since someone had been up here? Perhaps not for seventy years, since the Valentines had been small children.

I definitely didn't want to fall through, but I was curious. Cautiously, I continued up. I caught a glimpse of light at the top, and after a few more steps, entered a sparsely furnished room. The light came from an oval window in the dormer. There was a nightstand that held a pitcher and a bowl, and hanging above it, a small rectangle mirror. I walked over and swiped its surface with my hand. A dusty version of myself stared back.

This had to be the nannies room like I suspected. I turned to see her bed, just a tiny cot. It was lumpy and unmade, with a faded quilt thrown over in a heap that half hung on the floor. How odd, seeing how neat the rest of the room was.

Something about the lump on the bed caught my attention. It looked eerily in the shape of a body.

Outside, the gardener struggled to get the lawn mower to start, the engine turning over and over. Finally it caught with a cough. The familiar rumble gave me a sense of security, and I walked over to the bed with my shoulders back. Seriously, I was being silly. It was just an unmade bed. I could even see the top of the pillow.

I reached out for the corner of the quilt and ripped it back.

A smile stared up at me.

CHAPTER 4

I leaped back even as my brain scrambled for an explanation. The smile was decidedly toothy. Much too toothy.

Okay, I got it. This was one of those fake skeletons like my science teacher used to have in class. Mr. Dennis often dressed him in bow ties and hats. This one had its hand resting across his chest with a loose watch on its wrist. The watch was unusual in that it was encrusted with fake diamonds. He looked to be made of the same yellow plastic as my old Fisher-Price toys. Apparently, Kari wasn't joking about the skeletons in the house.

Who on earth would put a fake skeleton under the covers? Was someone trying to prank me? Was it Richard? Kari had warned me he thought he was a funny guy, and he did know I would be going through the rooms today.

I could feel my pulse start to hammer, and not in fear. Anger. This was *not* funny. I started to leave the room to give him a piece of my mind when something stopped me in my tracks.

Hair.

My brain finally computed that little detail. A few tufts, like brush bristles, clung to the skull.

Oh, no, no, no. I backed away, my feet flapping together in a tangle. Down I went on my backside. I pedaled backward like a crab as a scream began to squeeze out. My jaw dropped, but instead of a scream, loud coughs came out instead.

Dust from the floor clouded around me.

I crawled for the stairs. The wood was slick, but I ran down them anyway. I slipped at the bottom and clawed at the door frame for balance.

"Help!" I screamed. Dead eyes of the rocking horse stared at me. I scrambled for the door and flung it open.

Ms. Valentine stood on the other side of the doorway blocking my escape. I gasped, halfway sucking in my hair. She didn't react to my emotion as her steely gaze contemplated me with her lips firmly pursed.

"What are you doing in here?" she coldly asked.

"I...I was looking for you." My heart beat like a butterfly trying to escape a jar.

"There's no need for you to be in here. This is our playroom." Her eyes stared like she was trying to bore holes into my skull.

Something about the way she said playroom scared me almost as much as the thing I'd seen upstairs. I barreled out of the room.

"You should leave now," she said. "You don't belong here."

Her words sent chills down my spine. My brain swam in surrealness. Was this another time? Was I some naughty drunken guest who snuck up into the playroom?

I blinked hard and mentally shook myself. *What am I thinking? Get a grip, Stella.* "I've found something. It's up the back stairs."

Ms. Valentine's attention darted towards the rear of the room. Her gaze swept back and I felt I was about to be tossed out on my ear.

"It's a skeleton!" The words burst out of me almost in defense. Ms. Valentine raised an eyebrow as though I were incoherently babbling. I insisted. "It's lying in the bed upstairs."

Ms. Valentine turned and stumped down the hall. "Come along."

I watched her, stunned at her lack of reaction, before following after her.

"It's not real," Ms. Valentine said.

"It—" I started.

"It's Richard's prank," Ms. Valentine said, leaning on her cane. I swear I heard her knuckles creak.

A prank? I thought about the hair. "I don't think this is a prank," I said.

I followed her down the staircase with my mind spinning. Charity met us at the bottom. She'd changed into another dress.

"Time for pie?" she asked, hopefully.

"No," said Ms. Valentine firmly. "Have you practiced your piano?"

"Yes, sister, I did my lessons." Charity smiled proudly, oddly looking as though a child's face peeked out through an old woman mask. "Will we be having the party soon?"

I waited a moment to see if Ms. Valentine were going to tell her sister what I found. When she wasn't forthcoming, I shared, trying to carefully word it.

"We have a little problem," I said.

Ms. Valentine huffed.

"A problem?" Charity parroted back to me. The way she tipped her head made her look even younger. I regretted bringing it up.

"It's Richard," Ms. Valentine snapped. "Ms. O'Neil has stumbled onto one of his pranks."

"Oh! His pranks! Isn't he so clever?" Charity's feet tapped the floor, giving a glimpse of a pair of old Mary Janes.

"I'm afraid this wasn't a prank," I said. "I need to call my boss to let him know there's an issue." I used boss, rather than uncle, hoping it sounded more authoritative.

"What's the matter? Tell me, sister, what's the matter?" Charity pattered around Ms. Valentine like a little puppy.

"You can't possibly believe that," Ms. Valentine sniffed disdainfully.

"Where's the problem?" Charity asked, her sausage curls bobbing as she turned.

"Upstairs in the playroom." Ms. Valentine answered.

"Oh, momma said to stay out of there."

"Charity, dear, why don't you go check on Richard."

Stomping her foot, Charity walked away, I grabbed my phone and dialed Uncle Chris.

"Yellow," my uncle said, in that way that normally drove me nuts but right now I hung on to like a life line. It was the only voice of sanity in this crazy house.

"Hey, Uncle Chris, you know that house you wanted me to stage?"

"The Valentines?"

"Yeah, that one. Um, we have a problem." I lowered my voice. "I found a skeleton. You need to send someone out right now."

"Get off that phone. I'm telling you, that's preposterous," Ms. Valentine stamped her cane on the floor in an impatient staccato.

I tried to ignore her. She tapped me on the arm with the end of her cane.

I have to admit, I saw red. I nearly jerked the cane away from her. Breathing harshly, I had to walk outside because I wasn't sure what I was about to do.

"Stella? You there? Are you sure you aren't seeing things?" Uncle Chris asked.

When I reached the porch, I nearly yelled, "She just poked

me with her cane." Oh, boy. I needed to calm down. "You have to get the police here. Because I've about had it."

There was silence for about two beats. Then, "Of course, if you're sure..."

I was out to my car by this time. "Uncle Chris, it had hair and missing teeth. It was grinning at me." Prickles rose on the back of my neck, the kind that warned me I was being watched. Slowly I turned toward the house.

Ms. Valentine stood in the doorway. But that wasn't what freaked me out.

It was Charity in the upstairs bedroom window. For the first time, the silly grin had dropped off her face. Her eyes were narrowed and calculating. When she saw I'd caught a glimpse of her, she tugged the curtain closed.

Suddenly, I felt very alone.

"Uncle Chris," I whispered.

"Yes?"

"Can you come too? Like right now?"

"I'm on my way." He hung up.

I fumbled with the car door and climbed inside. After a second, I locked all the doors. *I'm silly. I'm so silly,* I told myself. But, I couldn't shake the fear.

From the doorway, Ms. Valentine glanced behind her like someone called her name. With a withering look in my direction, she slammed the door.

Who had called her? Richard? Charity? I panicked as I pictured them going up to the room and clearing out the skeleton. Would they do that?

They might.

My hands started to sweat. Should I go back inside? Guard the skeleton?

You have to stop. If they're the type to get rid of the skeleton, then they might get rid of you.

I called Uncle Chris again. "Have you called the police yet?" I blurted when he answered.

"Yeah, and I'm still on hold with them. I'm about halfway to the Valentine house, myself."

"Really?" Relief rushed through me.

"You better believe it. Your dad would skin me alive if anything happened to you. It might be the first family homicide."

"Don't even joke about something like that at a time like this." I shuddered. Seattle never looked so good.

CHAPTER 5

It was just a short time later that the manor's driveway was filled with police cars and the coroner van. The sun had disappeared behind the clouds, leaving the light dark and gray, with the ancient trees looming over the house like grave keepers.

I stood with Uncle Chris along with a group of officers in the Valentine's foyer.

"So you have no idea who that could be?" asked one officer.

"Obviously some vagrant broke in," Ms. Valentine said. Her lips creased into a thin smile. I was surprised her face didn't crack.

"A vagrant, huh?" said the cop, taking notes.

"Yes. You know, we never go up to that floor. It's been closed off for several years. We just haven't had the money for the upkeep of this house. We're on a limited income, at our age."

"Plus, it's freezing." Charity giggled.

"That's what I meant, Charity. We can't afford the heating bill for more than our personal living area."

The coroner came down the stairs. His two assistants rattled a stretcher as they followed him. On it was a black body bag, one that looked decidedly on the thin side.

"Are you sure it's even real?" Ms. Valentine asked, her eyebrows raised skeptically.

"Ohh, is that it? Is that the skeleton?" Charity asked.

"Yes, ma'am." The coroner nodded to Charity, and then to her sister, he added, "And, yes ma'am. I am absolutely sure this is a real skeleton."

"So, I just want to double check who lives here," said the officer. "It's you, your sister, and your brother Richard."

"Yes, that's correct."

"And that's all. There's no one else."

Ms. Valentine shook her head, but I noticed she tapped Charity on the foot.

"And you don't have any idea who that could be?" The officer pointed to the bag outside now being put in the coroner's wagon.

"No. I have no idea," Ms. Valentine said.

"Huh." The second officer chewed the inside of his cheek. "So you think a vagrant came in and fell asleep in your bed and died. That's your story?"

"Not in my bed," Ms. Valentine answered coldly.

"Right. Right. I mean a bed in the house." Despite his dubious tone, he leaned on his heels and smiled with a look of patience one often applies to listening to a preschooler telling a story.

"Really, just look at us, at our age. What other explanation is there?" Ms. Valentine folded her hands over her cane and sighed. The dim light from the cloudy sky washed out her pale gray eyes, making her pupils appear like pinpoints.

She also looked ageless. I don't know how. It was common knowledge that the woman was in her eighties. But she appeared strong and healthy with her thin body clad in an old-fashioned dress.

Ms. Valentine noticed me studying her and gave me a sardonic smile. Then she leaned heavily on her cane with a painful groan. Her face creased into its usual roadmap of wrinkles and her eyes widened in confusion.

Did I just see what I thought I saw? I squeezed my eyes tight. I must be exhausted or something. Maybe I needed vitamins.

Uncle Chris tapped my elbow, and I followed him out to his sports car.

"Wild, huh?" he said. He opened the driver's side door and dropped in.

"You're telling me," I said, standing outside the open door.

"I do seem to remember you saying you were up for an adventure." He cocked an eyebrow as he smiled.

"I guess I got one, then."

He laughed and then reached in his console. "Well, before you go home, you need to stop by the post office. I got a notice for a package for you." He handed over a pink slip.

I glanced at it and saw my name was scrawled across the address slot. What in the world?

"Okay, thanks."

"Get some sleep. I'll see you later." He waved and was off.

I got in my car and left while the cops were still talking with the family. Honestly, I was more than happy to make my escape.

As I DROVE BACK to town, it began to sprinkle, just enough to cause the windshield wipers to squeak against the glass.

The phone rang and my car announced it was Kari on the screen. I pressed the answer button. "Hello?"

"Girl, I just heard!" She was shocked, I could tell.

"Right?"

"Come meet me at Darcy's Doughnuts! You need a treat after that experience."

I met Kari at the local doughnut shop. My skin still felt shivery at the memory of Richard's smile. She was in a booth by the window, with a doughnut and coffee waiting for me.

I scooted into the seat across from her. "Holy cow. You needed to warn me. I didn't realize I was helping to sell the Addam's family mansion."

She took a sip of her iced mocha and her eyebrows raised. Swallowing, she said, "So, what on earth happened?"

"You told me to clean, so I was cleaning. Lo and behold, I didn't realize I had an audience," I said.

"I would have freaked."

"Yeah, well I can proudly say I did. I'm telling you, there is something weird going on with that family."

"Those sisters," Kari shook her head.

"Yeah, the sisters are strange enough, but have you met the brother? The other day he was standing behind the van like a zombie. Even his eyes looked lifeless. I swear, I almost ran him over." I rubbed at the goosebumps prickling my skin. Normally, I was pretty unflappable, minus my fear of spiders. Get a spider web on me and I'd dance around like some frenetic Ninja warrior. But the way his eyes had followed me had completely unnerved me.

What Kari said next didn't help. "They are a strange bunch. I remember telling ghost stories about that house when I was a kid." She picked off a piece of doughnut and shoved it in her mouth like she hadn't just said the word "ghost."

I swallowed. "Are the Valentine's dangerous? What did my uncle get me into?"

Kari laughed. "No, nothing like that. They aren't ax murderers."

"Did you just say ax murderers? You know we have a skeleton on our hands."

"I'm sure there's a reasonable explanation. It's just that

around here the brother is known as a prankster. Clear up until he turned sixty or so he was still pulling pranks."

Huh? Pranks seemed juvenile and along the lines of innocent. Pranks did not match up to his creepy eyes. "You mentioned that the first time we went there. After my discovery today, I'm thinking I need some more details."

"Oh, once he filled the memorial fountain with bubble solution. He painted a giant butt on the mayor's posters. Juvenile stuff like that. He'd been caught so many times that no one really knew what to do. It did no good going to the sisters. They ignored every negative thing said about him."

"What finally made him stop?"

"Well, the last time he was up on the neighbors roof. He fell off and broke his leg. That kept him quiet for a while." Kari shrugged and pushed her short blonde hair behind her ear. "You just need to stay business-like. Gladys Valentine is the high-brow of the family. She doesn't want anything to happen to tarnish the family name so you can imagine the hardship it's been on her having Richard as her brother."

I thought of the stiff-spined woman whose face seemed creased permanently into a disapproving frown. "No joke. She scares me. She was infuriated when I called Uncle Chris about the skeleton."

Kari dunked her doughnut. "I'd say that's about right." She

took a mouthful, then used her hand to shield her mouth. "But she thinks she's all Miss Prim-and-Proper and lives by manners associated with a century ago."

"Except with the practical jokes."

Kari nodded. "Except those."

"So tell me the scoop. Those three siblings live together, but none of them got married?"

Kari slowly shrugged. "There's a rumor there was a fourth. A boy."

My jaw dropped. "Don't tell me that's the skeleton?"

"I doubt it. I don't even know if it's true. I just heard rumors of a baby, but it was long before my time."

"A baby." Pictures of a little ghost baby flew through my mind. "One that died?"

She took a sip of coffee and set it down. "You know how town ghost stories go. I heard a rumor that the kid went off to be a roadie. Maybe he joined the circus. Maybe he wasn't real at all. After the mom died, that family kind of fell apart so who knows. Like I said, lots of spooky stories surround that house." She glanced at my doughnut. "You going to eat that?"

I shook my head and pushed it over. I never liked cake doughnuts, so it wasn't much of a sacrifice.

"Any more stories I should know about?" I asked.

She shrugged again. "I know one that used to haunt me when I was a kid was about the aunt. Apparently, she went crazy in that house. Used to talk about the Valentine sisters like they were ghosts."

My mouth dropped. "What?"

Kari laughed and shook her head. "Oh gosh, I'm sorry. I was just kidding. You should see your face. Honestly, it's just a weird old house owned by an eccentric family. You know how people are. They always make up stuff about things they don't understand. Relax. This will work out."

"Are we still going to sell it?"

"Of course, we're still going to sell it. This will all clear up and we'll be back on schedule in a couple of days. You'll see."

CHAPTER 6

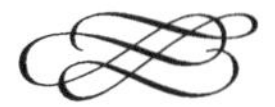

The rain had stopped by the time we were ready to leave. Kari had to go fill a prescription, and I thought I might as well pick up the package. This was as good of a time as any to acquaint myself with my new town.

Brookfield was cute, with fake old-time looking storefronts that kind of made me miss Pikes Place Market in Seattle. It had a mixture of old world charm like a place time forgot. *I bet these buildings looked the same back when the Valentine sisters were girls.*

I wandered down the street, my hands jammed in my pockets trying to get rid of the chill I couldn't seem to shake. Someone tapped me on the back. I turned around with a smile.

There was no one there.

I glanced around, confused. I know I felt something. I checked my shoulder and didn't see anything.

This wasn't helping my spooky feeling go away. I swallowed hard. *It was probably a raindrop.*

Biting my lip, I continued on. The post office was as quaint as the rest of the town, its brick front constructed to resemble an 1880's government office. I stopped to admire the big emblem at the convex of the building and then opened the door.

Immediately, I was hit with a blast of air-conditioning. Why they'd have this on, on such a drizzly day, I'd never know.

There was already a woman at the counter being helped. I got into line behind her.

The postmaster appeared to be somewhere in her late fifties. The pin on her blue sweater vest said Jan, with a golden eagle with outstretched wings encompassing her name.

"That's just terrible about your husband. Gout's nothing to fool with. Now, what was the zip code again?" Jan asked the customer.

The gal in front of me rattled off some numbers.

The postmaster punched them in her machine. She had a quirky smile that matched her short dutch-boy haircut. "Okay, that'll be twelve eighty. So did you hear about the Valentine place?"

The woman dug through her purse on the counter. "Yeah. Can you believe it? Who's going to want that place, now?"

It was obvious the postmaster wasn't in a hurry and was well-prepared to dish up a good slice of gossip by the way her eyebrows lowered as she leaned against the counter. "I don't know, but I'm sure that realty's going to squeeze every penny out of the sale. I heard O'Neil is courting some big developer."

"That realtor taking over all our house sales. They're wrecking our town! Although, honestly, it's probably best they tear that mausoleum down, anyway. Nothing good's come from there."

"That's true. But you might feel different when you see apartment buildings going up in its space."

The transaction dragged on while they discussed everything from the customer's new grandbaby, the weather, to how the Cash and Carry grocery store was raising its prices on milk.

Finally, it was my turn. I approached the counter with a big smile.

"And how can I help you today?" Jan asked, resting her hands against the counter. Thin rubber covered the tips of three of her fingers.

"Hello. I need to pick up a package." I slid over the paper my uncle had given me.

"You're new in Brookfield, huh? I'm Jan. I've been at this post office for nearly thirty years."

I raised my eyebrows to appear impressed. "Wow! That's amazing. You must really like it here."

"You name a place where I can have Skittles and my coffee breaks any time I want." With that, she jabbed her thumb behind her where I caught a glimpse of an orange tabby cat. Presumably the Skittles that she was referring to.

She continued, "Probably have a good ten years more before they kick me out of here. We'll see. They made McGregor retire last year." She sniffed as she walked to the back where metal shelves lined the walls. "He wasn't yearning for that, and he sure didn't like the nifty pen they gave him as a gift. They give me a pen and I'll show them where they can stuff it."

I had no idea how to respond to that. I hoped a polite smile and a murmur of agreement would do the trick. I didn't want to think about what I was agreeing to.

Jan lifted the paper to find the name. Her lips silently moved as she read the address and her body stiffened. I could practically hear the "Oh, crap," going through her head as she realized what she'd just said about my uncle.

Her eyes cut over to me as if she were trying to calculate just how much I'd heard. I smiled—what did I have to lose? She obviously knew the town. Might be good to see what else she'd share.

"Ms. O'Neil," she said, bringing the package up to the front. She placed it on the counter with a thump.

"Thanks," I said, turning the package a little to read the return address. It was heavy. Seattle. Of course. It must be from my dad. I could only imagine what was inside. I gave an indignant sniff that I could take care of myself, but deep down I was hoping there was a check inside as well.

"I see you're an O'Neil?" She drawled out the last name, her eyes dropping to the label as if having to reassure herself that she'd read it correctly.

"Yep. That's me." I didn't offer more to see what she'd say.

"So, you work for the Flamingo Realty, huh?" the postmaster asked, cautiously probing.

"Yep. Just got hired." Okay, time to pump for some information. Maybe if I gave her a little, she'd open up. "He's my uncle. I heard you talking about the Valentine house a minute ago. I'm helping out with the sale."

She blanched and I thought she was going to excuse herself. Then she rallied on, "Oh, do you have a buyer for it?"

"No. We're actually getting it ready for an open house."

"Open house! Huh. That sounds fancy. I bet that's keeping you busy." She hesitated for a second and then said. "How are you getting along with the Valentines?"

I really had to be careful how I answered this. What if she was friends with them? She'd seemed to defend them a bit with the last customer. "I don't really know them. Charity seems very nice. Are you friends with the family?"

She shook her head, making her gray hair swing slightly. "Those sisters are a good fifteen years older than me. Closer to my mom's age really. My mom's cousin had a debutante ball with them."

"Really?" *Give me the scoop. Come on.*

"That was quite a long time ago. Back near the Korean War. So many of the men were leaving."

"Did Richard leave?"

"Oh, Richard. You met him, huh? Of course, you have. You be careful with that one. Honest, it's amazing he's still alive."

"Why is it amazing?" I asked.

"He isn't exactly well liked around here. I'm surprised he didn't meet with some accident." She used her fingers to make invisible quotation marks. "But you didn't hear that from me."

I nodded, understanding the reasons why he wasn't well-liked. But that people might wish him bodily harm did surprise me.

My phone vibrated then. I pulled it out to see a text from my uncle. **—Need you to stop by sometime today.**

I slid it away. "Have you ever heard about a fourth child in the family? A boy maybe?"

"No, I never have. The family's had only three kids that I heard of. But you never know with all the gossip. Although those three keep us yapping enough."

"Do you know anyone who might have heard the story of a fourth?"

Jan gave me a suspicious look, so I hurriedly added, "With selling the house, it's important we know who all the heirs are."

That seemed to satisfy her because she nodded. "You can check with my cousin, Sharon. She works at A Cut Above. Don't let Marcy cut your hair though. She'll butcher it."

Considering Jan's old-fashioned style, I figured Marcy must really be bad. "All right. That sounds great. Now, is there anything else I should know? I kind of feel like I'm walking into the lion's den."

She laughed. "Oh, you'll find out soon enough."

What did she mean by that?

The bell rang over the door and Jan glanced up. "Good afternoon, Mrs. Everly! What can I do for you today?"

It was obvious she wasn't going to say anything more. I waved goodbye and grabbed up my box and left.

CHAPTER 7

Once on the street, I glanced down the block. I thought I'd passed a salon on the way here, one with a giant pair of pink fluorescent scissors blinking off and on in the window. I touched the tips of my hair. They were getting kind of crispy. Might be a good time to see if they take walk-ins. Ah, there it was. I left the package in my car and then headed over.

On the front window, a hand-painted sign in calligraphy said A Cut Above.

I entered, setting off a bell.

Sitting at the desk, a young woman with long black silky hair smiled as I walked in. "Good morning. Do you have an appointment?"

"No, I was just passing by and wanted to see if you had an opening."

The salon had six chairs, three on either side of the room. Sinks were located at the back. The whole place smelled of shampoo, with undertones of something chemical.

"What are you looking for?" She wrinkled her nose, just a tiny bit, as if she couldn't believe the state of my hair and she wasn't sure they were up for the challenge.

"Oh, I don't know. I was thinking a trim."

She glanced at the ledger in front of her. "It seems we do. Marcy?" she called over her shoulder.

I gulped. The one lady Jan told me not to use.

A red-haired woman popped out from behind a door of a room located at the back of the room. She wiped her mouth from whatever she'd been eating and gave me a once-over.

I shot out sweat like a porcupine does quills. "Actually, someone recommended I see Sharon?" I smiled apologetically.

"Sharon?" The receptionist look up doubtfully.

"Yeah. I was at the post office, and Jan told me to stop by."

"Sharon!" screeched the receptionist. "Someone asking for you! You have time for a haircut?"

"Just a trim," I added. It had taken me a long time to grow my hair past my shoulders. Eons, it felt like, ever since a near scalping I'd given myself in my senior year. Every time I grew it to my shoulders, it needed another good whack to get it healthy again.

An older woman appeared from the back room, her gray curls styled in a bouffant. She wore all black with a colorful plastic apron. "Sure!" Sharon said, waving to me. "Come on back."

She had me in the black plastic cape and my hair in the sink to shampoo my hair. "So, how do you know Jan?" she asked.

Water bubbled around my ears. "Just met her," I answered.

I could tell she was still talking, but I couldn't make out a word. I weakly smiled and closed my eyes, hoping she'd understand.

After a second, she sat me up and patted my hair with a towel. "Right this way," she said, her voice reminding me of the grandma on the pancake syrup commercial.

Soon, she had me in her chair where I was confronted with the reflection of a washed out version of myself looking like a drowned rat in the mirror, every blotch illuminated by the fluorescent lights.

"Just a trim, hun?" she confirmed.

I nodded, and she went to work, parting my hair with her

comb and flashing her scissors as she snipped. The beautician next to us had a victim in her chair, looking equally as miserable as myself, with foil in her hair.

"Well, I learned some interesting gossip," Sharon said to the other stylist.

"Oh yeah? Girl, after last night at the Drunken Cow, I could use it. What's going on?"

"You're getting too old to be doing that," Sharon clucked her tongue in disapproval.

"Hey, I've gotta have my fun!" the other woman laughed.

Sharon measured my hair in front. She did not look happy.

Sighing, she went back to whisking her comb through and snipping with lightning speed. "It's Susie. You know her?"

I watched in the mirror as the other hairdresser nodded.

"Sure do. That girl's got a mouth on her. Knows everything about everyone."

"You know the one. Well, she was saying she heard that house up on Bright Hill had the cops called."

"That Valentine one?"

"You got it."

I felt like ducking my head. It was weird hearing them discuss it right over me.

"And get this. There was a dead body found in it." Sharon raised her eyebrows knowingly. She knew she'd just dropped a bombshell.

"No!" gasped the other hairdresser. "You think it's one of their family?"

"I don't know. It could be that kid that stayed at the Valentines for a few months. He was my dad's good friend. His name was Kyle, and both him, my dad, and Richard used to be the town devils, I swear. Last that my dad heard of him, Kyle had shipped off to Korea with Richard."

"Oh, my gosh! Did he die?"

"I don't think anyone knows."

"Well, honey, who would voluntarily live with them? I once saw Richard shoot that light-up sign out on State road."

"That was him?"

"Yep." The other beautician blushed. "He said it was night pollution. I never told no one though. He caught me watching him and put his fingers to his mouth to tell me to shush. Honestly, I was too scared to say anything after that."

"I don't blame you. I wouldn't either.

The comb went through my hair hard, causing my head to jerk.

"Oh, sorry about that, hun," Sharon said to me. She spun me in the chair and brought out the hair dryer and roll brush. Quickly, she dried it and then turned me back. "How's that?" She lowered her face until it was next to mine, and beamed at me in the mirror.

I took in a deep breath and tried not to make a face. It was short, a lot shorter than I expected, with some weird layers.

"So much better!" she exclaimed.

Her partner chimed in, "Looks good!"

I looked so strange to myself I didn't know how to react. I smiled and thanked Sharon. After all, it would grow back some day, and I did get some interesting information. I paid and tipped and then headed back to my car.

So I had new information, but also new questions. Now I learned that Richard's friend had once lived with the Valentines before disappearing. Where was he, now?

CHAPTER 8

The sky was a stormy-gray when I walked out, like someone had pulled up a charcoal blanket over the town. The wind blew through my hair and sent shivers down my back. I still had to go over to Flamingo Realty to see what Uncle Chris wanted. As I started the car, I glanced at the box next to me. I could hardly wait to see what was in it.

Uncle Chris's secretary, Margo, was behind the desk, taking phone calls. She was a no-nonsense woman who liked to stare over the top of her glasses when she talked to you. She waved her hand as I came in, indicating I was free to go into Uncle Chris's office.

I knocked lightly.

"Come in!" he called.

I figured this was going to be about the skeleton, so I was a little surprised to see him standing with a four-foot tall flamingo.

He was smiling but his face went blank as he saw me. "What did you do to your hair?"

"What?" I touched it. It must be as bad as I thought. "Oh, just a haircut. Anyway, what was it you wanted?"

"Well, you look nice." His eyes winced as he said that. Then he glanced at the flamingo proudly. "Looky what I've got for you for tomorrow."

"What do you mean, tomorrow?"

"I just got word from the police that we're free and clear to have our open house this weekend. I insisted those cleaners come back tomorrow, and the Valentines have agreed to stay out of the way. I'll need you to babysit the cleaners and tack this bad boy in the driveway for advertising." He patted the flamingo with a smile.

I stared at him, this man who used to be a former race car driver, the rebellious young man who my father used as an example of not to go down the wrong path, this man with pictures of himself with girls in bikinis all over his walls. Yet, there was no doubt he was extremely pleased with the hot pink plastic bird in his hands.

"All these flamingos! What is it about them, anyway?" I asked, gesturing to the ones on the desk and in the windowsill.

"What do you mean? You know it's our logo." He smiled.

The flamingo had a cheesy smile on as well.

"That's great, Uncle Chris. But you never did tell me how a flamingo came to stand for your company."

"Oh, it's a long story."

I raised my eyes to meet his. "I'm here for the long story."

He glanced up, his round face pink and shiny with a sheen of sweat.

"All right, here it goes. We were at the speedway and it was Rock-n-Roll race night. I'd gotten drunk the night before at the Rusty Rooster—you know that place? Stay away from it. Anyway, in comes Michael Jacobs. Man, I hated that guy. He was there with his little posse, they thought they were something else, let me tell you. Some of his crew starts flipping my crew crap, and the next thing you know, it's about to be lit."

"A fight, huh?"

"Yeah. I was so drunk I was ready to take them all on. What

happened instead was he called me out. Called my car a plastic mod car. Took a few insults, and the bet was on."

"The bet?" I asked.

"He told me if I won I could have his car. But if he won then my motif had to be a giant flamingo. 'You have to paint your car all pink,' he'd said. I was such an idiot, I said yes."

I snorted. "I gather you lost, huh."

"Laugh it up, chuckles," he said, glaring at me. Then he smiled. "Yeah, you can say I lost. But I also won."

"Really? How's that?"

"Well, I lost that race, but it wasn't long before I was winning other races. And that pink car got me tons of notoriety. Everyone was talking about it. Pretty soon that's what people knew me for." He shrugged. "So when I started this business, it was a no-brainer. Do a flamingo. Go big or go home." He balanced the bird against the desk and sat down.

"Well, that's kind of a cool story. You made it work for you."

"Yeah, I did. You know why else it fits me? Because I'm single and ready to flamingo!"

I groaned. "No bad jokes. Don't make me put my foot down," I said and winked.

"What?" His brows rose in confusion.

"You know...flamingos stand on one foot...? Never mind."

"Ah, yes. Leave the puns to the experts, Stella." He laughed and then stretched back in the chair with his hands behind his head. "You're enrolled in real estate fundamentals?"

He was talking about the real estate school.

"I just enrolled in Association of Realtors and started my thirty hours."

"Great! Then you take the test."

I nodded.

"Terrific. Then I'm sure that the next house will be all yours."

"I'm kind of scared, to be honest, after this one."

He laughed. "Please. That house is over a hundred years old. It was to be expected to have a few skeletons in the closet."

I wasn't amused.

He stretched in his seat. "Besides, the story the old lady gave seems to be playing out. Someone broke in and died."

"They just broke in and died? That doesn't even make sense?"

He snorted. "You never know what kind of excitement this business is going to bring. I once sold a house, only to find a vault in the basement with a million dollars in it."

"Wow!" I raised my eyebrows, impressed.

"It was a legal pickle, I'll tell you that." His smile dropped off abruptly. "But seriously, what about you? You okay after finding Mr. Bones?"

"Yeah, I'm fine."

He twiddled his coffee cup in a circle, and studied me for a second. I could tell his desk hadn't been wiped in a long time from the dried trail of coffee circles on top.

"Ah, Stella." He sighed, and I sensed his mood changed.

"You okay?" I asked.

"You know, Stella, I've got some guilt. I always meant to check on you when you were growing up. You know, after your mom left...." His voice trailed off.

An urge hit me to ask him if he knew why she'd left, but then I realized I couldn't get that vulnerable. Instead, I leaned over and picked up a dead leaf from the floor and twirled it in my fingers. "I was okay," I said.

"It's just your dad—the way he up and moved away. I was so angry at him for that."

"You were?"

"Yeah. It was so selfish."

"He wanted a fresh start," I murmured to defend him.

"He wanted an escape. And not just from your mom, but from your grandpa as well."

I glanced up at him and was surprised to see his mouth turned down in pain. "How come you don't talk with him?" I asked.

He groaned and pushed away from the desk. "It's been a long time. Too long."

"They say it's never too late," I encouraged. There was a part of me that wondered if the family could get back together. Who knows? Maybe I could do it.

"That old coot wants nothing to do with me either, trust me. He's fine the way he is. Likes being alone, always has. Probably shoot anyone who steps foot on his property."

I bit my lip. That old coot was one of the main reasons I'd moved back. I was trying to work up the guts to meet him. Uncle Chris was deflating that hope faster than a pin to an air mattress.

"Well, you never know," I said, my gumption coming out like a whisper.

"Don't you be bothering about him. You have enough on your plate. Like a house showing." He nudged the flamingo toward me. "I'm assigning Kari to be with you every time you're there. Go in pairs. There's just a little too much weirdness going on at that place for either of you to go alone. Now, don't be finding any more skeletons, you hear?"

I was relieved at his decision, and gave him a little salute. That was a discovery I never wanted to repeat again.

CHAPTER 9

With his warning hot in my ear, I gratefully headed home. After a day like today, I was ready for some downtime to unwind. It was still misty outside, the kind that made me use the windshield wipers every twenty seconds or so. Not quite rain, but cold enough my defrost had to remain on to keep from fogging up.

I pulled into the driveway with a sigh of relief. Already, this little house was feeling like home.

I dropped the box on the counter and set a kettle on the stove. A minute later found me rummaging for the cup-of-ramen that I had. I found my favorite mug, the one my dad gave me when I won our state track championship in high school. On that day we'd experienced freezing rain, and he'd filled it with cocoa packets and marshmallows. I smiled as I saw it now—#1

Champ. He'd gotten one similar, with his emblazoned #1 Dad. So corny. Yet so special.

I didn't have cocoa but I did have some chamomile tea. I opened the bag just as the tea kettle started to spit. I filled both the mug and the styrofoam noodle cup, and then turned my attention to the box while they steeped.

I needed a knife to cut it open. On my way to the drawer, I caught a glimpse of my hair in my reflection in the kitchen window. Startled, I touched it. If this is how Sharon did, I can only imagine what Marcy's cut would have looked like.

I tried to pull it back into a ponytail, but it was a no go. Rolling my eyes, I tucked it behind my ears. It's a good thing I looked cute in hats.

Returning with the knife, I turned the box and sliced it open.

I wasn't sure what to expect. Maybe food? Hopefully money. I'd be grateful for either at this point, although I didn't want him to know that.

Inside was an envelope with my name printed in neat block letters. I recognized my dad's handwriting. Always crisp. Always precise. I took the paper, a fork and my noodles, and sat down to read.

It was only one page, which surprised me. Twirling up some noodles, I began to read.

Stella,

Miss you, kiddo. You being in Pennsylvania has brought memories that I'd thought I'd long forgotten. There is a part of me that hates that you moved. Yet another part sees an adventurous heritage. It's in your bloodline.

We never talked a lot about family, and that's my fault. I guess maybe that's why you're back there, looking for your roots. Well, here's one I wanted to share with you. Your great great grandmother, Wiktoria, escaped from Hitler during World War II. She came over on the ship, Wojtek, and requested asylum through Ellis Island.

She had to leave her mother behind. Through the years, Wiktoria wrote her letters. She didn't see her mother again until a month before her mom passed, when she flew back to Poland. She brought these letters home.

When I left my father's house, I took these letters with me. He was a family destroyer, and I didn't think he deserved anything of value.

But now, I'm passing them down to you. I know life is hard. There has been so much you've missed with your mother leaving, and your grandfather being the way he is. I want you to know where you came from. I want you to remember that through your veins pumps the same blood as a woman who ran from Hitler. You are strong. You are brave. I love you.

I've made many mistakes. I've given into my own emotions, despite how it may have affected you. Sometimes the flesh is weak, but the spirit is willing.

In the end, please know I've always loved you, and I've always been honored to be your father.

And because I know you well, I will end with the fact that no, I'm not sick. Be good and keep making me proud.

Dad

Ho boy. My bottom lip felt rubbery and my eyes stung like I was cutting a thousand onions. What was he doing to me? When did he get so soft? I reread the last paragraph and breathed out in relief. Yeah, he did know me. The first thing I would think of was that he'd gotten bad news from the doctor. Still, this was so out of his character I wasn't a hundred percent sure he wasn't lying.

I refolded the letter and searched through my childhood memories for signs of this sentimental man. My eye landed on my mug. I guess he was always there. I just hadn't seen him that way before, instead seeing him as a perfectionist. Maybe I'd spent so much time trying not to let him down, I'd missed his softness.

I thought about what he said about my grandfather and wondered if he hadn't looked at his father through the same lens, missing the good stuff about him. Uncle Chris couldn't come up with a good reason on why he didn't see his dad, other than too much time had passed. Both my dad and Uncle Chris were good men. It made me more hopeful about my grandfather.

I spooled up some more noodles and then began my search into the box.

There *was* food in there, which made me laugh. He was treating me like I'd gone off to college. But, since I was still waiting for a paycheck, it was a welcome sight. He sent cookies, soup, mac-and-cheese, and boxed hamburger casseroles. He even sent tuna fish. There was another envelope with a check in it, two hundred dollars, along with note that said crisply, "Had some spare cash. Get yourself some groceries, or shoes or something."

At the bottom were the letters that dad had mentioned. They were bundled in a stack and tied with string.

First things first. I sent Dad a text that said simply—**Thank you soo much! You are and have always been the best dad. I love you.**

Smiling, I pressed send. After studying the precious packet, I carefully untied the string.

My great, great grandmother. Wow. I smoothed the paper and then realized it wasn't going to be easy to read. Her handwriting was cramped. It was also written in Polish.

Oh, boy.

I took a sip of tea and thought about this. Then I went and got my laptop. I bet a translate app would help. Obviously, it was going to take a long time. Maybe it wouldn't even work. But my dad sent these to me somehow expecting that I'd be able to read them, so I wasn't going to let him down.

The computer screen blasted its homepage glare. I found the app and clicked on the original language box and switched it to Polish. Carefully, I tried to discern the letters of the first sentence and hen-pecked the keys one by one. I chose English for the translation.

I held my breath as I pushed enter.

My dearest Mother,

I punched the air in victory. Yes! I could do this!

My phone dinged. I picked it up, expecting a text answer from my dad.

It was from the moving company. A long apology on how there was a fire and the moving company would be delayed another few days.

I groaned and glanced down at my clothes. I needed to do something about this. Tomorrow, for sure, I'd stop at the store.

But for tonight, it was time to hit the washing machine again.

CHAPTER 10

The storm had settled by morning, and the sun was a soft white light hidden behind the mists of fog that had settled in the valley. I poured a mug of coffee and then pulled on my long cardigan. I checked on my socks that I'd left to dry over the back of a chair and, hopping on one foot, yanked them on.

Buttoning my sweater, I padded out to the front porch and curled up in the swing. After arranging the sweater so it covered my bare legs, I settled against the wooden back. The swing gently moved. I breathed in deeply, taking in the subtle sweetness the lingering blackberries gave off.

A flock of birds flew over head. I craned my neck to watch as they disappeared over the trees.

Drat. Speaking of birds, I had to go put that giant flamingo up at the Valentine house. Kari had called that morning, all panicked, to tell me that she couldn't meet me after all. "Stella! I'm so sorry! Christina has 103 temperature and the stomach flu!"

Of course, I'd told her to stay at home. She needed to be with her little girl. But on the flip side, it meant I had to go to the Valentines by myself. I was just a tad apprehensive.

After I left the house, I took a little detour on my way to the manor, to a road just outside of town. It was called Baker Street, and there were only two driveways off of it. There was a house hidden down behind the trees to the left. I'd never seen it, but I knew it was there. I'd been by this place many times before.

It was my grandfather, Oscar's home.

One of these times I was going to go right down there and knock on the door. I really was. I just needed to work up the guts first.

I idled past it and stared down the driveway. But, just like every other time, I couldn't see anything. Finally I gunned it and headed out of town.

I was nervous, and those nerves continued to build on my drive to the Valentine house. I pulled into their driveway and actually had to take a few deep breaths to calm myself. My chest had a tight feeling in a way I definitely didn't like. I sat there and breathed, and stared at their front yard.

The landscaper had gotten it under control for the first time since I'd been there. Weeds were pulled in the walkway and the bushes trimmed from covering the windows.

Not bad. Not bad at all.

If you liked looming houses with giant black windows and hidden skeletons in the attic.

I got out of the car and yanked open the back door. First, I pulled out the *open-house this weekend* sign from where it had been crammed behind my seat. I found the post that Uncle Chris had told me about and hung it up. Then I went back for the enormous flamingo. The thing was over half my height. I felt like we were in an awkward dance together as I struggled to get it out of the car and then sashayed with it down to the end of the driveway. Grunting, I jammed its metal feet into the ground next to the sign.

Finished. The flamingo stared drunkenly up at the sky. I shimmied it a bit to straighten it out.

A huge crow cawed overhead. I glanced down the street, realizing how isolated I was, even though I knew there was another house just beyond the corner. It was hidden behind the tall hedges that edged the property line. They closed everything in.

I shivered and turned toward the Valentine house. The windows stared back like the black sockets of a skull. It took everything I had not to picture a white specter peering from one of the windows. Maybe the one left behind from the anonymous skeleton in the upstairs room.

Okay, stop. You're staging in there today. There's no point in freaking yourself out.

Hmmm. I always knew I was nervous when I started to refer to myself in third person in my own thoughts. For crying out loud. I had to pull myself together.

I walked down the driveway and checked out the side yard. Something bright had caught my attention.

It was a metal roof.

Was it a work shop? I didn't remember anything about a shop being mentioned in the listing. I stood up on tip-toe, trying to see more of it. The building was quite a bit back there, nearly hidden in the trees. In fact, I would have missed it entirely if the landscaping crew hadn't trimmed some of the lilacs that had almost swamped it.

Wait a minute...was there someone walking behind the shed? Someone big, hulking. Someone carrying a shovel.

"Stella! Yooohooo!" Charity yelled my name.

I jumped. Charity hobbled down the porch, waving frantically.

I glanced back at the workshop, but there was no one there. Had I imagined it?

"Well, come on in, you silly." Charity waved a hand. She was nearly half-way down the driveway. "We've been waiting for you."

We? I glanced around the porch and saw the cleaning van was already there. I wondered if Denise, the one who'd abandoned me the first day, was back.

Charity was already returning to the house. How did someone with such tiny feet beat me?

I trotted down the driveway after her.

"What's behind the house, Charity?" I asked as I caught up with her. "By those bushes?"

"Hmm? Watch your step." She veered over a tree root that had grown through the driveway without even looking down, a display of muscle memory from years of avoiding it.

I had to admit, I was feeling out of breath. "The shed or workshop in your backyard. I don't recall Kari mentioning it."

She scampered up the stairs. Was she ignoring me or did she really not hear me? After all, she was in her eighties.

I followed up the steps after her. Ms. Valentine met me at the door wearing the same dress, or one identical to it, that I'd seen the other day.

"Hello. How are you doing, Ms. Valentine?" I asked.

"How am I doing?" She rolled her eyes.

"Yes." She was using even a simple question like that to kick me down. "I mean, with the skeleton and everything?"

Apparently, she didn't deem that important enough to answer because she responded instead with, "I presume you're here to finish what you started?"

"Y-yes." I straightened my spine. "I guess we're still having the open house this weekend. What do you think?"

"It's what needs to happen, I suppose, if we're to sell the manor." She glanced at the porch pillar behind me. Her eyes hardened, but in a shocking twist, her bottom lip quivered.

"Sister?" Short little Charity asked, her voice full of concern.

Ms. Valentine cleared her throat. "Let's get going, then. Not all of us have time to waste."

I nodded and started to follow her. Still, out of curiosity, I had to see what had caught Ms. Valentine off guard.

Squinting, I saw what appeared to be a carving of some type. I needed to remember to check it out better when I left later.

"So I trust you can get things together without causing any more trouble?" Ms. Valentine said over her shoulder.

My mouth dropped open. How was it my fault there was a skeleton in their house? But the way she stared at me... the color in her iris's nearly faded to a light blue-white. I shut my mouth and nodded instead.

"The cleaning crew showed up earlier. They're in there now." She gestured to a pair of ornately carved doors. "I thought you'd arrive with them and not force me to babysit."

"I'll keep an eye on them," I said.

She nodded and walked toward the kitchen, her cane rapping smartly against the floor. I rubbed the back of my neck and then opened one of the doors.

There were two women in there, vacuuming and dusting. A row of cleaning supplies lined up to the left of the door. One of the women glanced at me and I gave her a thumbs up. They had this covered. I figured I might as well help and grabbed a bucket.

The one vacuuming turned the machine off. It turned out she had headphones in her ears.

"You must be Stella," she said warmly.

"I am!" We shook hands, and the other woman joined us. I found out they'd been focusing on the downstairs windows and floors. I gave them my phone number so they could get hold of me if they needed anything.

"I'm just going to check the other rooms," I said, readjusting the cleaning bucket in my hand. They sent me okay signs before I headed out.

The rest of the doors in the massive downstairs hallway were closed. I glanced at the stairwell, wondering where the Valentines had disappeared off to.

I stopped outside the room Ms. Valentine had earlier indicated was the library and sucked in a deep breath, a little afraid of what I might find. Well, there was nothing for it. Might as well get the job done.

"Let's see what's behind door number one," I whispered in my best game host voice and wrenched the knob open.

A thrill ran through me. It was like entering into something out of Alice and Wonderland. Bookshelves fifteen-feet-high lined three of the walls. Dust motes danced in the light and a heavy scent of old paper permeated the air. One wall was curved, with floor-to-ceiling windows. Underneath was a window seat covered in tufted green velvet.

I was charmed by the fireplace and a rolling ladder that rested on its ancient rails. I walked over, conscious of stepping quietly, and gave the ladder a little push.

It rolled a few feet. I tested my weight on its lower rung, and then climbed up a couple steps.

I couldn't keep the smile off my face. I was surrounded by more books than I could read in a lifetime. Antique books bound in leather, their titles embossed in gold print, stood primly together. I wondered if they'd ever left the shelf after they'd been placed there.

One book stood out on the shelf in its uneven height compared to the others. I glanced behind me. No one was there. Feeling like a little kid, I reached for it.

Graceful embossed script rose over the leather cover saying *King James Bible*. I knew people recorded their family trees in these. Excitement raced through my veins as I realized the heirloom in my hands. Quickly, I climbed down, holding the treasure like it was a nest of frail bluebird eggs.

I carried it to one of the leather chairs and sat. The book rested heavily against my knees. Gently, I opened it.

A puff of dust accompanied a crack as the cover moved against its spine. On the first page was a graphically detailed illustration. I sucked in my breath.

It was a picture of a wailing person. Man, or woman, it wasn't detailed enough to determine. But gripping the person's heel was a claw, and below that, flames and evil laughing faces.

I shuddered and turned the page. The next showed a depiction of Eden, with the same evil smile beaming from a serpent curled around a tree branch.

I flipped to the next. Finally, this one was marked Family tree. I snuggled the book closer to read.

The calligraphy penmanship had the depth of dipped ink. In swirls and slashes, it wrote out a series of names. I silently read them, assuming they were grandparents and parents, until I came to Gladys, and Charity.

Richard Valentine's name was there as well, but interestingly, in a different colored ink. The writing appeared cramped in comparison with the gorgeous curls above.

Below those three, the family line stopped. It was almost an insult to see all the empty lines underneath their names.

The room suddenly felt colder and I shivered, wishing I had on my sweater. I flipped through the rest of the Bible's pages. It opened naturally to where there was a letter hidden. I couldn't help my grin as I pulled it out.

The paper was frail and appeared like it had been torn from something else. I gently unfolded it to read,

Dear Diary,

The Winter Ball is tonight. I can hardly wait. Sister and I are getting ready. She keeps scolding me for laughing, but I can't

keep my bubbles inside. It's snowing heavily and Bently has stoked all the fires. It will be a warm, intoxicating night. There's enough snow outside, I wonder how many guests will come by sleighs. I love hearing the bells when they arrive.

The words ended there, with no sign of who had penned them. I carefully folded the note and replaced it. Thoughtfully, I continued to search through the pages.

Excitement hit again when I discovered a picture about halfway through. Although it was faded to a deep sepia color, I could see it was a picture of the Valentine family.

There were six.

The room became colder still. I glanced up at the fireplace and wondered if that was where the icy chill came from. Frowning, I held the picture up to see it better.

The baby wore an old-fashioned dress and bonnet and sat on his mother's lap. Next to him stood his adult sisters, Gladys and Charity. Charity's finger was being clasped by the young baby, while Ms. Valentine leaned slightly away from her sister, her lips pursed together as though she'd just bitten a lemon.

Mr. Valentine stood behind his brood, with Richard by his side. Richard wore a suit or perhaps a military uniform. Perhaps this was taken right before he went to Korea. I remembered then about his friend, Kyle. Sharon the hairdresser had said that Kyle had lived with the Valentines for a short while before being shipped overseas with Richard.

I started to slip the photo back in between the pages when I saw there was a scripture heavily underlined. Curious, I read it.

Behold, I was shapen in iniquity; and in sin did my mother conceive me. Psalm 51:5

What the heck? Scary stuff there. I replaced the photo. Gently, I riffled through the rest of the pages of the Bible but there was nothing more. The chill lingered, trickling around my neck like an icy scarf. I stood up to climb the ladder to put the Bible back.

Once that was done, I glanced around and tried to assess where to start cleaning. It had gotten so dark outside, and inside as well. Was another storm brewing? The only light was emitted from dim gas lanterns hanging overhead. How curious, who had even lit them? This would never work. I could barely see. I needed to find a light switch.

I felt along the walls, richly covered in wainscoting and tapestry paper, but I couldn't find the switch. I passed the open door and noticed that, even in the hall, the light was much darker than I felt it should be. Cold air rushed through the doorway.

It was then I heard it. A high, tinkling laugh.

Every hair rose on my neck.

It didn't sound like an adult woman's laugh. It sounded like a child's.

I pushed the door closed. It slammed shut and the supporting walls creaked. I backed away. I could hear something else.

Music.

I turned to the curved window, searching for the sound. My heart pounded when I realized I'd never seen a bay window from the outside. Where was I? I walked closer, trying to map out exactly where I was in terms of the front the house.

Above me, the oil lamp flickered and went out.

I recognized the music now with a shudder.

Sleigh bells.

CHAPTER 11

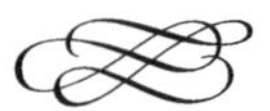

I clapped my hand over my mouth, cutting off a scream. What was happening? Fear ran through my veins like icy scorpions. I'm not paid to deal with ghosts. No way! I've got to get out of here!

My hand was slick with sweat as I tried the doorknob. I tugged as hard as I could but the door refused to budge. Almost like it was mocking me. I took a step back, my mind screaming at me to be rational.

I heaved in a breath, trying to listen. The chills now turned into sweat that ran down my face. Was the house being super heated? Was I going crazy?

I heard bells again. I swear, it drove every last rational thought from my mind. I pounded on the door, screaming. "Help!"

There was a scratching by the doorknob, and then it slowly turned. I backed away. My hands balled into fists, ready to defend myself.

The door cracked and slowly swung open. I grabbed it and yanked it the rest of the way, breathing like a locomotive.

The tall figure of Ms. Valentine stood on the other side, her lips pressed primly together. Her eyes immediately narrowed.

"Ms. O'Neil?" she said in a harsh whisper. "What is the meaning of this?"

I don't care. I don't care. Just let me out of here. I dashed around her and into a very brightly lit hallway. My heart thumped as I tried to get hold of myself. Like a man sleepwalking, I turned to face the library.

"I—uh—I couldn't get the door to open." Even with fighting to be calm, I sounded hysterical to my own ears.

"Ms. O'Neil. This is an old house. The doors can stick at times. Kindly just knock and someone will come let you out. There's no need for all that commotion."

I swallowed, my mouth dry. Lamely, I tried for an excuse. "I needed a light for this room."

Her eyebrow arched as she studied me. The seconds of silence grew. Finally, she whirled around and marched into the room. She snapped on a switch. Sconces along the walls brilliantly shone. She turned back to me. “I’m sure you’re acquainted with a light switch?”

I stared where she had turned it on. That hadn’t been there before... or had it? “I saw the gas lamps and thought that maybe....it went out.”

“You thought we didn’t have electricity?” She sniffed. “Richard merely lit the lamps earlier to test them. The realtor mentioned buyers might like the old-fashioned lighting. It’s been ages since they’ve been used. I’m surprised they work as well as they do.”

My pulse slowed even as my cheeks heated with embarrassment. I nodded and then smiled. What on earth had I been thinking? That I’d been caught in some time warp? I could only imagine what she thought of me.

She eyed me now. “Is there anything else?”

I shook my head.

She smiled then. My heart leapt to my throat. The grin showed nearly all of her teeth, the corners of her lips curling up into her cheeks. I swear she looked just like the illustration of the serpent.

I stumbled back, which made her laugh.

With that, she turned, “If that’s all, I will be going now. I need to oversee Charity’s practice session.”

So that was it. Charity was practicing music again. Probably something with bells. I'm such an idiot. I shook my head. Honestly, that skeleton must have really done a number on me subconsciously. I'd never been so jumpy.

Ms. Valentine hummed as she walked away.

Jingle bells.

The skin on the back of my neck prickled. Okay, that was enough for me. I gathered my cleaning bucket from the library and called Uncle Chris. He didn't answer, so I left a message. "Hey, the flamingo sign is up and the cleaning crew is here. Everything looks under control, so I'm headed out."

That was the truth of it. I wasn't returning here again until I had Kari with me.

It only took ten minutes of drive time with the sun's glare on my windshield for me to feel ridiculous. I was letting all those crazy stories get to my head.

They were a creepy family for sure. But that skeleton was the curveball. Who was it? Could it be the young man, Kyle, who had lived with them temporarily? I mean, the guy just disappeared.

How would I go about finding the answers to something like

that? I chewed my thumb. Maybe I could drop a call to the police officer who'd interviewed me that day I found the skeleton.

And what happened to the baby? Now I knew he wasn't a rumor. I saw him with my own eyes in the picture. Was Kari's story correct? Had he grown up only to run away to the circus? Maybe I could poke around and see if I could find out more.

In the meantime, real life was still happening, and I needed to pay rent. Since this day was kind of a bust, I called my landlord to see if I could drop off the check.

Gaila Crawford and her family had lived in the area forever. Actually, this visit could really work for me. Surely, she knew the Valentines. She was in her seventies or so, herself. Perhaps she went to school with the three siblings.

Even more on my mind was if she knew about the baby.

I pulled over to the side of the road and found her number.

It rang and rang. An uneasy feeling made me wince as I wondered if I should wait for the answering machine, or if I had now entered the annoying territory of letting the phone ring too much.

"Hello?" A pleasant woman's voice came through the receiver.

"Hi, Mrs. Crawford? It's Stella. I'm out and about and wondered if I could drop off my rent to you, if it wouldn't be a bother."

"Collecting money? No bother at all." Her voice hinted at humor. She rattled off her address and then ended with, "Though I suppose I should give you a deduction after the toilet fiasco. Is everything working well now?"

I assured her it was.

She continued, her smooth voice bringing to mind one of Hollywood's old time starlets, "It's a little bit of a drive. I'll see you soon."

I quickly mapped her address and saw she lived about twenty minutes in the opposite direction. I popped the radio on and spun the car around.

It turned into a beautiful day, one of those dog days of fall that began with the bite of cold but warmed up to unseasonable levels later in the afternoon. It was such a welcome reprieve after the storms we'd had.

The directions took me to the left down a dirt road. Acres of green fields welcomed me into the rural farmland. A cloud followed behind my car, announcing to everyone for miles around that I was on my way.

I had to say, dirt roads still caught me by surprise. Out in

Seattle, most of the roads were paved, outside of a few logging roads or county transfer roads.

Mrs. Crawford's house sat on the pinnacle of a rolling hill like the star jewel on a crown. I was searching for the driveway when I spotted a bright red object out in the middle of the meadow. It kind of hypnotized me, being so unexpected. Then I saw it move.

What the heck?

As I got closer I saw it was bell-shaped. And closer still proved that it was an umbrella. I realized it was Mrs. Crawford wandering her field, shielded from the sun by a giant red umbrella.

My phone beeped a command that I'd arrived. I pulled down her driveway and braked, the car softly jerking at the stop. I rummaged through my purse and grabbed the check.

A breeze, carrying the warm scent of dried grass, lifted my hair as I climbed out. I sniffed deeply. It was interesting how every area had its own bouquet. To me, Western Washington was all ocean water and blackberries and fresh. It was fresh here as well, but different. I breathed in again, taking it to the bottom of my lungs as I walked out into the field.

Insect buzzing came from all directions in the grass. Grasshoppers jumped in front of me and tiny bugs clouded together in the sunlight. I had no idea what they were and held my breath as I walked past them.

After a moment, I noticed my pant legs were wet. Around me were white nests housing spit bugs. That nearly made me halt my journey altogether, until I noticed Mrs. Crawford was moving farther away.

I took a few steps to the left where I saw a path had already been cleared, presumably by Mrs. Crawford herself. I was about halfway there when she turned and saw me.

"Stella, is that you?" she called.

The sun was in my eyes. I shielded them and could see her peeking out from underneath her umbrella. She wore a flowing white shirt and matching pants.

"Hi, Mrs. Crawford." I waved and trudged forward.

She walked in my direction, her pace much more leisurely. When I reached her, she was studying the horizon with a small smile on her face.

"Look. You see down there?" Her chin raised in the direction.

I turned and saw a dark smudge in the distance.

"That's where I spent every afternoon during the summer." She moved her umbrella back and allowed herself a quick peek at the sky. "Yes, the sun was right about there, and I didn't leave until the sun sank low enough to kiss the ground." She smiled at me, flashing strong white teeth. "Now, how are you this afternoon, Stella?"

"I'm good."

"Are you?" Her brows slightly pursed together.

I don't know what magic powers that woman had, but I swear those two words nearly undid me. Was it finding the skeleton? Missing my life in Seattle?

She didn't say anything more, just kept those soft gray eyes focused on me.

Finally I'd pulled myself together enough to shrug. "Everything's great. I love the little house."

"Oh, that little house." She started walking forward again. "It's quite the special place. It was my first home, and I even came back here when I was married. Years ago, of course."

"Really? That's so interesting."

"Mr. Crawford was a museum curator up in Pittsburgh. He was quite a bit older than myself. Of course, you'd never know by how he chased me in those days."

The grass softly swished against the fabric of her pants.

"So, you never mentioned why you moved here," she murmured.

"Oh, I didn't? It was for a job."

"Yes, you mentioned a job, but not the real reason."

I stopped again. "How do you know these things?"

She softly laughed. "Oh, darling. It doesn't take much to know that a person doesn't pack up and move cross country for a job at a realty office. Not that I'm short-selling our beautiful state. Pennsylvania is amazing. But I figured it was something else."

"Okay," I laughed.

She let the question slide. "So you have my rent money, do you?"

I handed her the check.

"And how do you like your new realty job?"

"It's been...interesting. I'm helping to sell the Valentine Manor."

"Well, my goodness. They practically threw you to the wolves, didn't they?"

"You know about them?"

She smiled and twirled her umbrella slightly. "Darlin', you'd be hard pressed to find someone who didn't, around here."

I hesitated for a second and then blurted out. "I found something there. Something horrible."

"Do tell."

"It was a skeleton stuck up in the nanny's bed."

"Well now, they always said there were skeletons in the closet but that's taking it a bit literally."

"Ms. Valentine said she thinks it was someone who broke in." I bit my lip, kind of afraid to continue. "I have a crazy theory. There's rumors of another brother who joined the circus. I wondered if they were referring to a young man named Kyle who lived there at one time. No one seems to know where he is."

She hummed, "Mmm, I know what you're going to say. You think those could be long lost Kyle's bones."

"Yeah! Do you think it could be?"

"I think it's most certainly not." She gave an emphatic nod to punctuate the thought.

My mouth dropped. "Are you sure? I mean, it fits..."

"I'm positive. In fact, I have a little secret to tell you." She lowered the umbrella. "Why don't you come inside for a glass of ice tea."

CHAPTER 12

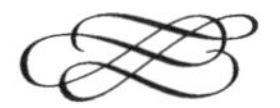

Mrs. Crawford walked up her porch steps. She skirted a planter filled with lush ferns and opened the screen door.

"You thirsty?" she asked.

Well, after that last comment, I sure was. I nodded.

"Come on in. I have some fresh lemon cookies I just made this morning. Heaven only knows why I do that to myself. After a certain age, a woman has to watch every bite. But as luck would have it, you can help me eat them."

I smiled and followed her into the house.

It was cool inside, painted a soft blue. White wood trim wrapped around the doors and windows. The floor creaked as

I walked, a comforting creak. The kind that says, it's been a long day and you're home now.

"Shall we eat out on the sun porch?" she asked. "Might as well take advantage of the sunshine while we have it."

Of course, I nodded. She was already leading the way to a large screened room filled with white wicker furniture. Hanging baskets of flowers decorated the corners. She flipped the switch for an overhead fan, its blades four white palm leaves, and then gestured to a chair.

"I'll be right back," she said, her caftan top flowing softly with her movement.

I pulled out a chair and briefly admired the floral cushion. The room looked out onto the meadow we'd just traveled through. It was cooler in here. I heard a sound of bells, which momentarily made my heart leap. But a quick look around identified them as a small set of wind chimes.

"So." Mrs. Crawford breezed back through the doorway. She had a tray in her hand with two ice-filled glasses of tea. She set it on the table and I saw a few powered-sugar lemon cookies sitting on a plate. She settled into the chair across from me and took her glass.

"There's some sugar on the tray if you need your tea sweetened," she said.

I lifted a frosty glass and took a sip. I tried not to pucker. It did indeed need some sugar.

She laughed and nudged the sugar bowl closer to me. As I stirred in a spoonful, she leaned back in her chair and looked out into the meadow.

“It really is lovely this time of year,” she reminisced.

I nodded.

“Please, have a cookie,” she said.

I grabbed one and, since she was watching closely, took a big bite. “Mmm, so good,” I said. And I meant it.

“Wonderful. It was my mother’s recipe. She used to make it on days like this.” She took a sip and set her glass down. “I promised you a story.”

Excitement hit me, possibly fueled by the sugar. Finally, I was going to get some answers.

“So, I know the skeleton can’t be Kyle’s.” She smiled, just a tiny one. I held my breath. “Because I knew him quite well.” Her finger ran under a turquoise necklace she was wearing.

“You knew him?”

“I most certainly knew Kyle. I went to school with him. He was a few years older than me. He may have been a bit smitten with me.”

"Do you know where he went?"

"Oh, that man. After the war, he was like a piece of crumpled paper that flew where the wind took him."

How do I bring up the obvious in a way that won't offend her? I bit my lip, and then began, "But it's possible that he may have returned home. Maybe he didn't let anyone know?"

She chuckled. "Well, anything's possible." Her finger went under the necklace again. "Except that I've heard from him recently."

Every nerve on my body jumped at her words. "What?" I managed to squeak out.

"I did. And I have this to show you."

She reached into her pocket and held out a little porcelain squirrel. The figurine was not more than three-quarters of an inch high.

"Cute," I said as I took it from her. I glanced at her questioningly.

"He gave it to me in high school, many moons ago." She smiled. "It was supposed to be my good luck charm. I had a test in chemistry that week. He knew I was worried and told me it would help me pass."

"And did it?" I asked.

"Oh, I don't know if it helped. I did narrowly squeak by. But I had so many other worries at that age." She flashed me a grin. "Like who to invite to the Sadie Hawkins dance."

"Did you invite Kyle?" I set the squirrel down.

"No, and that was part of my worry. You see, I had a crush on the band leader—I always had a penchant for those nerdy, brainy types. And I didn't want to lead Kyle on. He understood, I think."

"So, you heard from him recently?"

She nodded. "I did. Just a quick note asking how I was. There was no return address, but it was stamped from Morocco."

"Really. Did you think it was odd to hear from him after all these years?"

"Oh, at our age you tend to reminisce, maybe get a little nostalgic about the past. You start having more friends die than are living, and you want to check in on the living ones. So, no, I didn't think it was strange. Rather, I thought it was nice to hear from him."

"Was that the first time you'd heard from him since high school?"

"No, he used to write me a long time ago. And I'd write him back, just chatty letters about where life was taking us. Then there was the time I saw him for a minute about ten years ago.

He said he was passing through." She touched the turquoise necklace. "He said he wanted to give this to me. I often wondered if he was checking in on me to see if I was still married." She shook her head sadly. "I was, but I lost poor Mr. Crawford a month later."

"I'm so sorry."

"Oh, it's fine. It was a long time ago. The living keep on living."

I nodded. "Did you tell anyone? Maybe the Valentines?"

"Now, why would I do that when they were the very reason he left our little town?" Her gray eyes widened. "That would betray the very fabric of our friendship."

"I'm sorry. Of course, I understand. But, can you tell me, what it was he was escaping, exactly?"

She smiled again. "What do we all run from? Ghosts from the past. He was married once. It ended in a disaster."

"How did Kyle end up living with the Valentines?"

"Kyle lost his parents as a senior in high school. Mr. Valentine saw a lot of promise in him and brought him under his wing." She shook her head. "I often wonder if he regretted that. Kyle was quite wicked."

"Wicked, huh? That's a strong word."

"Strong? Well, honey, everyone around these parts knows that Kyle was a troublemaker."

"I've actually heard that it was both Richard and—"

"Oh, *that* man." She made a face. "He comes driving like a crazy person up and down this road. I heard tell he likes the way the car catches air when he races over the hill, but who's to know, really? Stay far from him."

"I'm trying," I said. "He shows up at the oddest times." I decided to ask my big question. "While I was there, I saw a picture of a fourth child. A baby. Do you know anything about him?"

She glanced at my glass. "Have you finished?"

The question was so abrupt and worded in a way that I wasn't sure if I was being dismissed or if she wanted to give me a refill. I confess, my mouth dropped open.

Then she turned away, and her forehead creased in such a way that she looked worried. I realized that maybe the subject of a baby was off limits for some reason.

I stood up. "It was so refreshing. Thank you. Well, I better get going. So much to do and so little time."

She chuckled. "I wasn't rushing you out. It's nice to have company out here on the farm." Still, she stood when I did, and lightly set down her napkin. She reached her hand out to mine and I thought she wanted to shake. So it was with some surprise when I saw the little glass squirrel in my palm.

"I want you to have this. It may bring you some good luck in selling that old Valentine place."

"Aw, are you sure? It's so special."

"No, no. You take it. I have a feeling you might need all the help you can get."

"Thank you," I said. I examined it quickly and then tucked it into my pocket.

She started toward the door and I followed her.

Casually, she said, "Now, I hope you have a good day. Let's do this again next month. I've enjoyed it immensely." She opened it for me and stood back.

I flushed, pleased to be invited back again. "Absolutely!" I stepped onto the porch and stuck my hand into my pocket, feeling the squirrel.

"And maybe then you can fill me in on what you're escaping, yourself." She smiled again and then slowly shut the door.

CHAPTER 13

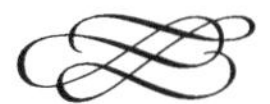

I headed to my car with the squirrel in hand, hardly believing that Mrs. Crawford gave it to me. I jiggled it and then tucked it in my pocket.

It wasn't quite dark out. Still, I flipped on my headlights because it was that weird in-between stage. Carefully, I backed out the driveway and turned onto the road.

The sky was a soft blue-gray with the sun a dark orange ball on the horizon. Trees flashed by like black shadows. It was so gorgeous out here. What really amazed me was how *country* the country was. There were no house or street lights that broke the darkness of the woods or fields.

As I drove, Mrs. Crawford's question replayed in my mind.

The first one she asked, the one I ignored and she'd hinted at again.

Are you running from something?

I'd always prided myself on being reserved. Pride was a good choice, because it was something I really couldn't change about myself. I watched people carefully to see if they were trustworthy. It wasn't hard for me to get a red flag.

I didn't share what I was dealing with in life, not really. My dad was a *pull yourself up by your own bootstraps* kind of guy. He had drilled into me to keep those emotions bottled inside in case someone saw you as weak.

I said that I moved to Pennsylvania for a new beginning. That was the safest answer, and one that my uncle, Kari and even my dad accepted.

Heck, it was the truth. I chose Brookfield, Pennsylvania because it was a place I could rebuild my life and still have family around. Dad suspected my grandpa was part of that equation. I didn't deny or confirm that to him. That was still a safe assumption.

But, after a series of bad relationships, I knew that I was running away from something. Me. And it was part of the reason I needed to connect with my grandfather. Call it an identity crisis, or just a breakdown, but one morning I found myself at work, all buttoned up in my business suit, caramel macchiato with light syrup-hold the cream in my hand, and I realized something.

I didn't like who I was.

So running here was trying to figure out what was important to me. I wasn't so sure how it was going, though.

To distract myself, I thought about the picture I'd found with the baby in it, and what Mrs. Crawford had said about Kyle. He was a troublemaker, huh?

Headlights flashed in my rearview mirror, making me squint. *Nice having your high-beams on, buddy.* I flipped up the mirror.

And, Kyle had been married before. Interesting. It was nice getting details about him that fleshed him out, to know he was a real person. I wonder how long he'd lived with the Valentines. It sounded like it was not long. And then both Richard and Kyle had joined the military. I wondered if they'd both joined right after school.

I glanced in the side mirror. The car was right on my bumper. What was this guy's problem? I checked my speed limit. I was already doing five over. I stepped on the gas pedal. I didn't want trouble on this dark road.

He sped up as well.

"Go around me, you idiot," I said. Why wouldn't he? There was no other car coming. No one around for miles.

My turn was coming up. I flipped the blinker, thankful I could get off the road and away from this guy.

I slowed and the car slowed, inches from my bumper. I floored the gas and turned the corner. *Get me away from here.*

I rolled my shoulders after I turned, my foot still pressing the gas pedal. Just get me home.

Every hair on my neck stood when I saw the headlights turn after me. Wait. He was following me? Who lives down this road? Like no one but me.

I sped up, and he matched me. I couldn't see what kind of car it was. The mirror showed only blinding round headlights.

My heart pumped hard. *I can't go home. What do I do?*

Dark shadows sucked the remaining daylight. It chilled me to realize I really *was* in the boonies.

I flipped open my map app on my phone and hit locate. It showed where I was on the road. There was a town a few miles away.

The road looked like it meandered deep into the country. I didn't see anything close by that could help. I thought I remembered there was a turn-around up ahead. Did I dare take it? What if he trapped me?

I was just going to have to drive to the next town. I couldn't risk getting blocked in.

The car got so close I thought it was actually going to bump me. I dialed 911 in a panic.

"Operator, how can I help you?"

"I'm being chased right now on English Elm road. It's some kind of road rage. I'm all alone."

"We have a car in the vicinity. Keep calm. We're on our way."

The headlights bounced off the side mirror and nearly blinded me.

"I'm afraid he's going to ram me!" I squealed, stomping on the gas. *What do I do? What do I do?* There was no one around.

"Just keep calm. The Sheriff's on his way."

Keep calm was easy for someone to say a million miles away all tucked safe in a cozy office. It was not something I could do right now. Adrenaline pumped through my veins like it was going out of style.

We passed a turn-around. The car behind me inched even closer and slammed on its horn.

"Mother of—" I exclaimed.

It hit its brakes and backed up until it reached the turn-around, then spun around toward the direction we'd come from.

My hands shook.

"Ma'am? Are you okay?"

"I—uh—the car just turned around."

"Did you get the make or model?"

"No, I couldn't tell. I just know it was a car."

"Was it a two-door or a four-door?"

"I don't know. I don't know!"

Was it Richard? He's known for driving in the area.

"Where are you now?"

"I'm heading home." I quickly rattled off the address. She assured me an officer would be by to take a statement. I barely heard her. All I could think about was who was that?

CHAPTER 14

I pulled down my driveway. To say that I was slightly shaking would be like saying the ocean was slightly wet. I was trembling so hard I could barely get the key to fit in the door lock. I hardly knew what to do with myself once I was in the house. I locked the door and checked it, and then turned around in search of a weapon.

I seized a knife from the butcher block and stared at it like it was a snake. What was I thinking? I couldn't stab someone. I threw it in a drawer.

Headlights came down the driveway. I ducked down behind the counter. Staying low, I crawled over to the window and peeked out.

It was a cop car.

I bolted up and unlocked the door.

The officer parked and climbed out. He was monstrously tall, looking to be nearly seven feet. "Stella O'Neil available?"

"Yes. That's me," I said, trying to control my trembling as I tucked a hair around my ear. Just seeing someone who represented safety made my eyes sting after the terror of what had happened earlier. I took a deep breath and crossed my arms.

"I'm Officer Carlson. We have a report that you were involved in a road rage event?"

"Yeah, uh. Come in." I stepped back from the doorway and the cop entered. He was in his mid-thirties, and when he took his hat off I could see he shaved his head. Whether by choice or balding, I wasn't sure, but his scalp was tan like he'd been doing it for a while.

He followed me through the tiny living room to the attached kitchen where I filled a mug and microwaved it for tea. I needed something to hold. I wasn't going to be able to maintain control of my nerves without it.

The officer cased my house really quickly before pulling out a notebook. "Can you tell me what happened?"

"I was driving home and this guy pulls in behind me." The

microwave dinged. I added a tea bag and clutched the mug, wanting the warmth to warm my bones.

"Where were you coming from?"

"From North Fork. My landlord lives up there."

His eyes raised toward me with a flicker of interest so I continued. "You know Tonya Crawford?"

"She's your landlord?"

I nodded and took a sip of my tea.

Officer Carlson made a note and continued. "So you were saying that someone pulled in behind you? A male?"

"Uh, I actually couldn't see who was driving. I guess I just assumed it was a man."

He nodded and scribbled some more. "So this car just pulled in behind you? Or did you pull out in front of it?"

"No, actually I was on the road first. I don't know where it came from." I frowned, thinking. "Actually, I think it came out of a field. Like it had just been sitting there."

"Mmhmm. And why do you think he was in this field?"

My heart filled with alarm as I looked at him. "I don't know? No reason, I guess."

"Hey, you aren't the realtor that is up at the Valentine's house, are you?"

"Yes. Yes I am."

"You're representing the house where the skeleton was found?"

"Yeah, I'm the one who found it."

He shut his book and stood a little straighter. "This isn't some publicity stunt, is it?"

"Publicity stunt?" I had no clue what he was talking about.

"You're trying to get a pretty penny for that Valentine Manor, I heard."

I frowned. "I hardly think finding a skeleton or getting chased by someone in a car makes the house more appealing."

"You never know. You're from the west coast, right?"

How did he know so much about me? "Yeah. So?"

"I've heard about those Hollywood types."

Okay, this was becoming laughable. "I'm from Seattle and not a real big shaker in the film industry."

"Ahh, came here to try and escape the rain, then?"

If he was going to go with that, so was I. "Yep." And since he'd already brought it up, I thought I'd continue. "About that skeleton, I haven't heard if they've come close to identifying it yet?"

"Not that I've heard of. Except they know it's a male. And, apparently, it had a chipped front tooth and a nice watch." He shrugged. "Still researching dental records to help identify it."

I shivered. Just a John Doe in the morgue. This was somebody's son, now a black bag and a toe tag that said nameless.

It would be burned in crematorium.

"We're still investigating the Valentine's story that it was an intruder who got hurt when he broke in. The house was so huge. Maybe he overdosed."

"And somehow crawled into the bed?" I asked.

"There's stranger things in this world," Officer Carlson said. "Anyway, I'll keep my eyes out. Maybe ask a few people if they've seen a loitering car. You let me know if you think of anything else."

With that, he headed out to his car. But as soon as his headlights left me surrounded in complete darkness, I raced to bolt the door.

It was then that my phone rang. I picked it up and read the name, grimacing.

It was my dad.

I was so shaken I didn't know if I wanted to avoid him or if I needed him now. With a deep breath, I answered. What little girl doesn't need her daddy?

"Hi, Dad,"

"Hi, Sweet Pea. How are you doing?"

Lie. Lie. Lie. He will freak if he finds out. "I'm doing good."

He paused and then said, "You don't sound good."

"No, just a crazy day at work." I could hardly stop rolling my eyes at my lies. "Did you get my text?"

"I did. So you liked the package?"

"Dad, it was amazing. Thanks for everything. Especially your letter. I'm going to probably keep it forever." I smiled.

"Oh, great. You're going to roll it out every time I tell you to get a better job, aren't you?" He teased. "Well, your uncle better be treating you right."

"He is."

"That little twerp better not be talking bad about me."

"No, nothing bad. Just that you are a little bit of a perfectionist."

"Perfectionist, nothing. Sometimes you have to put the work in to get where you want." He sighed. "Stella, how are you really doing down there? I've been worried."

It took everything I had to continue to keep the shakiness out of my voice. "It's going good. My house is cute. I like my new job."

"You have any inkling at all to move back? It's not too late, you know. I can still get you that great job."

"I know, Dad. I really want to do this." My voice dropped. "I need to do this."

"It's your grandfather, isn't it?" It was the first time he officially voiced it so point blank that I couldn't wiggle around the question.

"Why haven't you ever contacted him?" I asked. It seemed fair to get his reason right out in the open, like I had with Uncle Chris.

"You know I did it to protect you. Growing up, we were always moving because he had to protect his identity. He was always doing what was right, but we were the ones who had to pay. I lost friends, my own extended family. I was always moving from school to school. Mom begged him to quit. He would never listen. The FBI was his life. Then my mom died. He did that to us. Stole her. Stole a normal life my brother and I deserved."

I felt a pang of loss for my dad. I could hear it in his voice that he really struggled. I also could hear unforgiveness. I recognized it, that bitterness. It was a poison you took hoping the other person would die. It hurt me to realize my dad was in that place.

"It's not just me," he continued. "Look at your uncle. He's never contacted him again, either."

"I think Uncle Chris might regret that," I said, slowly. "Do you have any happy memories with your father?"

He paused and his breathing became labored.

I sank down to the sofa, hoping I wasn't pressing too hard. But I had to try. "He's been out of the FBI for a long time. What if he's changed? What if he misses you?"

He cleared his throat and exhaled. His voice was muffled as he answered. "Yeah, well. It is what it is. Sometimes there's no going back."

He was hurting. I had to ease up. "I love you, Dad."

"Love you, too."

"Thank you for the letters."

"Oh, yeah. Did you like those?"

"You know, they're all written in Polish," I said, dryly.

He laughed. "I figured a smart girl like you would need something to do on those long boring nights out in the middle of nowhere."

"You just wait. I'll figure them out, and then you'll be sorry," I teased. "I'll probably find out I'm heir to some big castle overseas."

"That'd be just my luck," he groaned. And then, more serious, he added, "Just...be careful, okay?"

"I will, Dad."

"Sleep well, Stella."

That night, when I went to bed, I thought about Dad's warning to be careful. I knew he meant with Oscar, my grandfather. But I took the knife with me instead.

CHAPTER 15

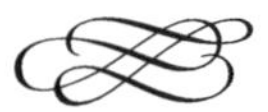

As my alarm went off, I sat up straight in bed, remembering that today was the open house. The next moment found me dashing to my closet, furious with myself for not making it to the department store yet.

So do I want to wear this dirty shirt, or that one? Obviously neither were going to work.

I drove to the bakery and grabbed a couple dozen cookies, the whole time chanting "I'm late. I'm late," like I was the white rabbit from Alice's Wonderland. Then, I jetted to the department store where I was strangely attracted to the signs that said "Clearance." I ended up rustling together an outfit that would have made any elderly aunt proud.

One pair of pink pants and floral shirt later, I was parking the car next to the old carriage house at the Valentine Estate. I grabbed the cookies, brochures, and a few realtors cards. Kari had told me to scatter the cards on the counter so it appeared like there was a lot of interest.

Heaving a calming breath, I climbed the porch steps. But before knocking, I remembered that carving on the pillar. Ms. Valentine had looked in that direction with tears in her eyes.

I found it right off. There was a heart carved into the wood. It looked like there use to be initials, but they appeared to have been gouged out. Interesting.

I knocked on the front door and waited. After a moment, the door opened and Kari met me with a smile. Her blonde hair was tucked into a cute updo, and she wore a pink business suit. We looked like the pink express, I swear.

"Hello, there!" she grinned cheerfully. "Cookies? Oh, boy!"

I wasn't sure what to expect from the last time I'd been there, but the house was clean and smelled of vanilla.

Charity ran up after her. "Hello! Hello! It's a party. Oh, it's been so very long since we've had a party."

Ms. Valentine thumped in behind her. "We're selling the house, Charity. The party isn't for you. In fact, it's no party at all."

"Well, I see cookies and flowers! It seems like a party to me!"

"And look what I have!" Kari waved a red canvas basket with a sign that said, "Please wear over your shoes." Inside was filled with paper booties.

Ms. Valentine stared at it. "Am I supposed to be impressed?" she sniffed.

Kari wilted, just a tiny bit. Then she rallied like a pep leader. "No, I just wanted to reassure you that we were going to take good care of your place." She turned to me, "Stella, will you come help me get some more stuff from my car?"

Of course, I'd help her if it meant I wasn't alone with the sisters. I set the cookies on the buffet and followed her outside. Her minivan was parked behind an enormous flowering bush.

"So, are you ready for the open house?" Kari asked as she slid open a door. A fast-food cup rolled out. She scooped it up and chucked it back inside.

"I really can't believe we're still going through with it."

"What do you mean?"

"I mean, what kind of people live with a skeleton and don't even realize it?"

"Even worse." Kari looked a little green.

"What?"

"No one smelled him."

Oh lawdy. My stomach flipped like a pancake on the griddle.

"I'm sorry," Kari said. "But have you thought of that? Crazy, right?"

"Maybe they have a bad sense of smell?" I offered. The other possibility loomed that they simply hadn't cared.

"I guess that's possible. And it was on the third story, in the back. They said it had been years since they'd gone up there."

"You think he entered through the vent in the attic?"

"I have no idea. I honestly don't have a better theory." Kari shrugged. "All right, lock all of those creepy thoughts up tight. Right now, we need to get this house sold."

I nodded. That's right, focus on the job. I could ask more questions later.

We carried the treats up the porch and walked inside.

Ms. Valentine watched from the side of the entryway, her hand on her cane. "I supposed this is for the pomp-and-circus you have planned?"

"Yes, that's right. We're going to get your house sold. That's the goal, right?" Kari breezed past Ms. Valentine. I hesitated. I didn't feel like I had the space to do it.

Ms. Valentine stared me down like a dog guarding a bone. Finally, I sidled past and galloped down the hall after Kari.

Thumping from Ms. Valentine's cane followed us.

"Okay," Kari said, eyeing the countertop. "It looks good in here. Let's set up."

"How long are these shenanigans going on for?" Ms. Valentine asked.

"Oh, an open house is usually an all day event. I suspect we'll be here until five or so." Kari looked up with concern, her forehead creasing. "You are planning to leave, right? You three have plans for the day?"

"Plans?" Ms. Valentine echoed, lifting her chin.

"Yes. Plans. Unfortunately, homeowners aren't usually present during these events. But trust me, I will have everything under control."

Ms. Valentine harrumphed. "And what happens when my prized china vase falls off the pedestal and breaks?"

"I have Stella here to walk through the house with any interested buyers. I've hired a few more attendants. And Mr. O'Neil himself has mentioned he will be stopping by. I promise, there will always be someone here keeping an eye on things. You did lock up everything valuable, like I told you, right?"

"Ms. Missler, everything in this house is valuable. Right down to the spoons." Ms. Valentine pursed her thin lips.

"Well, they're in good hands," Kari shot back, smiling gaily. It was the fakest smile I'd seen.

"I'll see you at five and not a moment later," Ms. Valentine said. She stared at me, her eyes feeling like they were trying to penetrate to my very soul. It took everything I had not to shiver. I smiled back.

Ms. Valentine was not impressed. She left the room, muttering. A second later, I heard her calling for her sister.

"Geez, I feel bad that you've had to deal with them all week," Kari muttered as she pulled the plastic wrap off the tray.

"You have no idea," I agreed. I looked for an outlet for the coffee pot and plugged it in. A second later, I had it filled with water and it began to do its happy percolating burps.

I heard the front door slam and then a car rev up. I walked outside to take a peek.

Ms. Valentine was in the passenger seat of the old T-Bird. At the wheel was her brother, Richard, with Charity peeking over his shoulder from the back seat. Richard backed up, with Charity looking like she was talking a mile a minute.

I jerked at the sight of the car. The grill looked just like the one on the car that had followed me the night before.

I ducked back so they wouldn't catch a glimpse of me. After a moment, I heard the car tires crunch down the driveway, and then it was quiet.

"Phew!" Kari said, her voice enthused with relief. "Glad they're gone."

I nodded and headed back to the car for more flowers. Kari followed me. We stuck baskets of them on the porch steps and a huge vase on the kitchen counter. Then Kari stirred the pot of vanilla something she had steaming on the stove. It smelled amazing.

"Potpourri," she explained. "I tell my clients to never ever use room deodorizer because it can turn off potential buyers."

The stuff on the stove had a nice soft scent, a mixture between cookies and fresh bread. I left her in the kitchen to go do simple things like straightening cushions and opening blinds.

It was about half-past nine when the doorbell rang.

"Our first potential buyer," I said with a smile.

"Don't get your hopes up," Kari answered. "At this time of the morning, most of the foot traffic is probably looky-loos. Can you imagine a house like this with such a history finally being an open house?"

She opened the door and exclaimed, "Ah, my extra help!"

Two young men appearing to be in their late teens or early twenties entered. They glanced around sheepishly while Kari explained to me. "I put out a hiring sign at the local college. I figured we needed to make sure anyone in here doesn't make off with the fine art or something."

She clapped her hands. "All right guys, if you can just hang out upstairs. Your job is to accompany people without looking like you're spying on them. Can you do that?"

They nodded and walked up the stairs, heads swiveling as they tried to take in everything.

Let's hope there were no more skeletons.

"Have you been up there?" I asked Kari.

"Up...?"

I bobbed my eyes toward the ceiling.

"Ohh. You mean where they found Slim."

I groaned at the nickname she gave the skeleton. "Well, yes."

"I did go check it out. Everything appears to be in its normal dusty mundaneness."

"So I'm safe to wander around?" I was curious about that skeleton, but preferred not to run into zombies, thank you.

"You want to wander?"

"I just want to acquaint myself better with this huge place. My last visit was kind of cut short. I ended up having a headache." Yeah, it was a lie. I didn't feel like going into the whole jingle bells creepy-crawly feeling right now though.

She laughed and waved her hand. "You go right ahead. Be sure to answer questions if you see one of our many looky-loos. And keep an eye out no one fills their pockets."

"You got it," I said. And then, sucking in a deep breath for courage that she'd never understand that I needed, I headed down the hallway.

CHAPTER 16

As soon as I walked past the library doors, a shiver the size that would be caused by a spider dropping on my head ran through my body. I didn't think I was brave enough to go in there alone, again. I quickly headed up the stairs.

They were so solid they didn't even creak, despite their age. The banister's finish was worn away at key spots from where hands repeatedly grabbed it, but it had a lemon scent from polish. The two college students peeped over the stairwell. When they saw that it was me, they went back to their conversation.

"Everything okay?" I asked as I passed them.

"Yeah," said the first, while the second guy interjected, "It's kind of freaky up here, isn't it?"

"Oh? It's just an old house." I laughed, trying not to sound nervous. "What's going on?"

He rubbed the back of his neck and then pointed down the hallway. "There's a weird noise coming from that room."

Dear heavens. Slowly, I turned in the direction he was pointing as every hair on my neck stood upright, like soldiers at attention. A long line of doors stared back at me. I swallowed hard. Was he referring to the one at the end? The playroom?

I held my breath to listen. There it was. I could hear soft banging coming from the third door down. And was that...music?

I released my grip from the handrail, where I realized I'd been hanging on for dear life and straightened my shoulders.

"I'll go check," I said, exhaling a deep breath. I was done with this and ready to confront whatever had been haunting me. As I marched, I fumed. I was done with being scared.

Of course, having two people watching me, ready to spring to my side if I needed help, supported my bravado.

At the doorway, I glanced back. Scratch that. The two young men hovered around the top of the staircase like they were ready to jump down the whole flight, depending on what I unearthed behind the door.

That's fine. I'll take care of it myself.

I wrenched open the door with a yell, "Hello? Who are you?"

The room was quiet and dark. A window shutter gently banged against the house siding in the breeze.

I ran over and grabbed the window shutter to pull it closed. Outside, a small wind chime hung from a branch. I smiled at seeing the source of the music. There, all that fear for nothing.

I wondered why the window was left open in the first place? Maybe the cleaners did it?

Slowly, I spun around to make sure everything appeared as it should. Not that I would notice anything missing.

A sheet shrouded the bed. There was a chair and a desk in the corner, and an ivory-colored dresser.

I walked over to the dresser and was charmed to see a worn pair of saddle shoes tucked out of the way. I wondered whose room this used to be.

The desk was a roll top. I hesitated for a second and then carefully pushed it up. It was rough, and the rumbles vibrated through my arms. It took a little bit of persuasion but it soon rolled back into its compartment.

There was a blotter protecting the wood surface, covered in tiny ink splotches. A nest of drawers stacked against the back, along with a few shelves.

My eyebrows lifted at what was placed in a line on one of the shelves.

Little glass figurines. Like the one that Mrs. Crawford had given me.

I picked one up and studied it. A tiny elephant. The glazed porcelain was cool to my palm. I carefully placed it back. Gently, with my finger, I opened a drawer. I realize I was beyond snooping. But this mystery had me so sucked in. Who were the Valentines?

There were several papers inside. On top was a newspaper article. The headline spoke of a debutante ball to be held at the Valentine Manor. Underneath it was a black-and-white picture of eight young women, all dressed in white. I flipped it over. There was a list of names, including Gladys Valentine. All these people who were friends with her. How did she end up so alone now? Marla, Mary, Pauline—these were her friends.

Underneath that picture was another photo, this one of a wedding. I recognized Gladys as one of the bridesmaids. She wore a long dress with a very unhappy expression on her face.

In shaky, thin handwriting across the back it said, Marla Springfield and I.

Marla Springfield. I'd heard of that name before. It took me a second when I remembered there was a Springfield Diner on main street. Was Marla or her family a part of that?

Suddenly, a cold chill went up my back. I held my breath to listen. The house was silent. The feeling grew, heavy and oppressive. Every instinct told me someone was watching me. I swallowed and carefully slid the pictures back in the drawer. The skin burned on the back of my neck. I pushed the drawer shut and then, slowly, turned to look behind me.

Nothing.

The door slammed shut.

I screamed and ran for the door. There was pounding in the hall and the door opened just as I reached it. One of the college students stared at me, his eyes wide.

"You okay?" he asked.

My heart beat in my chest like a dove frantic in a cage. "The door shut by itself."

He stared hard at me, then glanced down. His cheeks flushed

and I realized he was embarrassed. It took a second later to register he was feeling that way for me.

He cleared his throat and then mumbled, "Yeah, uh, someone came in downstairs. I guess when the front door shut, it created a vacuum." His eyes met mine briefly. "These old houses are drafty. But creepy, to be sure. I can see why that scared you," he added.

I closed my eyes. Took a few deep breaths. Counted to five. "Well, I guess I was on edge since you said you heard noises coming from this room."

"Did you figure it out?" he asked, glancing around.

I walked back to the desk and gently rolled the top down. "The window was left open and the shutter was banging. I closed it." I checked it again. "It's kind of strange though. I wonder who left it open. The Valentines said they don't even come up here."

He groaned. "The job description said this would be an easy couple hours of work. It didn't say anything about ghosts and weirdness."

I could see how this house was affecting him. His face was pale. In fact, he unbuttoned his collar and puffed his cheeks like he was feeling overheated from nerves. The last thing I wanted was for him to freak out and leave. I needed him here for my own security. I smiled confidently and said, "Oh, we're fine. Like you said, old houses are weird. Kari probably opened it earlier to air it out. Besides, no ghost would want to take you guys on."

He rolled his eyes as we walked out into the hall. His buddy glanced from over by the stairwell. "Everything okay?"

I nodded. Just then, Kari's voice rang up the stairwell. "And up here, we have more bedrooms than you can shake a stick at."

I realized she was leading potential buyers to this floor to check things out. I plastered on my professional smile.

But that cold feeling still lingered.

CHAPTER 17

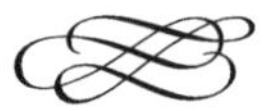

That afternoon, we had more potential buyers stop by than a dog had fleas on a hot summer day. Although, how many were looky-loos, as Kari called them, was hard to say. Retired people came through who'd once had dinner there, or remembered a holiday celebration. I heard similar comments over and over. Things like, "Remember how brightly lit this was on Christmas Eve?"

"Remember the dances?"

"Remember the celebrations?"

Remember, remember, remember. That word was repeated in something like eighty percent of the conversations. Every time I heard it, I'd smile and nod, and try not to feel discouraged. I was so ready to have this house in my rearview mirror.

We said goodbye to the last potential buyer at a quarter after four. I gathered up the shoe booties, the cookie trays, and the pitchers of juice. Kari ran the electric broom around. We both wanted to get out of there before the Valentines returned.

As we cleaned up, I asked Kari if she'd ever eaten at the Springfield Diner.

She was enthusiastic in her response. "Definitely! You going to stop by after this?"

"I was thinking about it." My stomach growled to tell me it might be a good idea.

"They have the best hamburgers. Still the original owners." She packed up the coffee machine.

"Really?" I wiped off the counter.

"Yep. In fact, Marla still works there, if you can believe it. She's this peppy old gal that knows everyone. I remember my grandparents taking me there as a little girl, and they'd chat so much, she'd forget to take our order. It will be a sad day when she retires."

Those words energized me more than any caffeine drink.

A car rumble roared outside to announce that the Valentines

had returned. I finished packing the box. "You care if I take this outside and then head out?"

"Go ahead. Thanks for your help today! Open houses aren't usually as crazy as this. But like I warned you, I knew it would grab the interest of people who've been dying to see the inside of the famed Valentine Manor. Anyway, have a good night."

"You, too," I said.

"Hey, and get the bacon burger! You won't regret it!" she called before the door shut completely behind me.

The Valentine sisters were slowly making their way out of the car as I hurried over to mine. I really didn't want to have a conversation. Instead, I waved my hand and sent them a smile, only to be received by a blank stare by Richard.

I shivered and climbed into my car. It was cold tonight, and the seat was like ice. I blasted the heat and shifted the gear. As I drove down the driveway, I glanced in my rearview mirror.

He was still staring at me. But what really grabbed my attention were his car headlights.

Round, like I'd seen following me last night.

It was him!

But that was crazy, right? How could he have known I was going to Mrs. Crawford's house?

Things were getting weirder and weirder.

I drove into town and up to the Springfield Diner. The outside restaurant lights highlighted flower boxes that hung from all the windows. As I walked up to the entrance, I saw they were filled with red geraniums. I loved red flowers. Not just geraniums, but dahlias, Transvaal daisies, and poppies.

I yanked open the door, noting how smooth the brass loop handle was from all the customers who'd come in before me. The atmosphere was cozy inside, not brilliant from overhead fluorescents, but illuminated by tiny hanging lights covered with small, caramel-colored glass shades.

I waited a moment, wondering if this was one of those places where you seated yourself. The restaurant was filled mostly with the older crowd. Even at this time of night, the scent of coffee was strong, and the conversation muted, mixed with the comforting sound of clinking forks on plates.

After no one showed up, I spotted a booth and seated myself.

A moment later, a waitress came by. She appeared to be in her mid-forties, with her bleached-blonde hair harshly pulled back into a ponytail. She set down a glass of water and a menu.

"Can I get you anything to drink?" Her apron was dirty and she smelled of hash browns. The tag on her shirt said Tammy.

"Uh, no. I think I'm good. But I was wondering, is Marla here?"

Tammy frowned with a hand on her hip. She clearly wasn't worried about her tip. "What'cha want to talk to Marla about?"

I was a little taken back by her defensive reaction. I could hardly say that I'd seen Marla's wedding picture at the Valentine house. I opted for subtle instead. "I'm new in town. My friend, Kari Missler, mentioned that Marla might be someone I'd like to meet." Yeah, I'll admit it, I name dropped. Hopefully, it would work.

She narrowed her eyes at me, and I smiled nervously back. I was just about to give up when there was a ding from the back. A man barked, "Order up!"

The waitress finished placing the napkin and fork in front of me. "I'll let her know. She might come out, she might not."

I nodded as a warm flush of relief filled my chest that the weird stand-off was over. "Thank you."

She rattled off the specials and then sashayed to go pick up the order.

I opened the menu, now completely uncertain if I wanted to

stay. I glanced toward the back and saw Tammy talking with the cook. Her hands waved animatedly and I could only imagine what she was saying. I wasn't sure if I was even welcome.

But, to my surprise, a few minutes later an older woman came out. She looked to be in her eighties and had on a flowered apron and a hair net. I was taken aback to see she was still cooking.

"Hi, there, young lady. I heard you were asking for me," she said. She leaned against the table on a bony hand, her knuckles poking out like lumps of clay.

"Hello!" I smiled, caught up in a strange feeling that I was being graced by royalty. "Thanks for coming out to talk with me. I can see you're busy."

"Oh yes." Marla glanced around and nodded. Her voice was gravely, like she'd spent many years with a cigarette going nearby. "We are busy. Been busy since the doors opened, nearly fifty years ago."

"Wow! That's impressive." I smiled and stuck out my hand. "I'm Stella O'Neil, by the way."

She shook it. I was surprised by how soft her hands were. "O'Neil. O'Neil," she rolled my name over her tongue, as if trying to taste what it was that it reminded her. Then her eyes cleared and she clasped my hand tighter. "You're the one up on the hill. Selling the Valentine's place? I've seen that flamingo of yours popping up all over these parts."

"Oh, thanks. Business is good, I guess."

"Yeah, the people are selling out. It's a shame."

A prickle grew under my collar. I swallowed. "I can imagine you've seen a lot of changes around here."

"Mmhmm, honey you have no idea." She eased some of her weight off her feet by leaning against the side of the table again.

"Did you know the Valentines?" I asked.

"Well, you sure could say I did. Went to school with Gladys Valentine."

"I, uh, I saw a wedding picture of you."

"You did?" Her eyes narrowed.

I nodded. She wasn't looking so friendly all of a sudden.

"Hmph. I didn't think there was any left of those," she murmured.

I wracked my mind, trying to find a way to suggest that she might be able to get a copy of the photo from the Valentines, when she blurted out, "Wish that one would burn too."

Uh oh.

"That boy was nothing but bad news." Her mouth puckered in distaste. "I couldn't be rid of him soon enough."

"So you got a divorce?" I asked. "That must have been hard."

"We weren't even married a year. I divorced him while he was away in Korea."

Interesting.

"I was best friends with Gladys. Of course, that ended badly too. In the end, I had nothing more to do with the Valentines. Not my fault. They just wouldn't talk to me. Even Mr. Valentine looked awfully sheepish when he saw me go by." She sighed. "I remember him helping my ma change a tire years ago, when I was a bitty thing. Thing was so bald it was practically a rubber band held together by threads. He ended up buying a new tire and everything. Wouldn't take a dime for it." Marla shook her head. "He was a good one, but he was never the same after his wife died."

She was best friends with Gladys Valentine? Why had her friendship ended? I nodded, sympathetically. "I'm sorry."

"Don't be sorry. My ex was a cheater and I was better off."

The kitchen dinged the bell. Marla glanced back that way and then at me. "Sounds like you have a little more digging to do. I like you. Spunky. Inquisitive. But be careful. You may be curious, but you ain't a cat. You don't come with nine lives."

She patted me on the shoulder. On the last pat, her hand rested. "I mean it, I'm warning you. The Valentine's aren't people to mess with in these parts."

The bell dinged several times in a row. "I'm coming! I'm coming!" Marla hollered. Then to me she muttered, "Calling me like some busboy. Geez, you'd think I didn't own this place." She continued to complain as she tottered back.

A few minutes later, the waitress returned. I ordered the bacon burger Kari recommended, along with a basket of fries.

While I waited, I grabbed the local newspaper that someone had left behind. I opened it with a smile. I remember reading the Sunday comics with my dad. It was one of the few times he'd let his hair down. Peanuts was his favorite. Mine was Calvin and Hobbes. Dad never understood it. "Is the tiger alive or not?" he'd ask.

"Dad, he's alive to Calvin," I'd try to explain.

He'd shake his head and grumble something about how comics had gone downhill since he was a kid. But give him a comic about Snoopy flying his doghouse and he'd crack a smile.

I flipped it to the front page where the headline proudly announced, "Missing hiker found safe after four days." The article immediately grabbed me with its first line, stating a hiker had been found in the National park. It got me thinking if there had been any missing persons filed around this area. How long did it take a person to turn into a skeleton? Wrinkling my nose, I grabbed my phone and typed it in the search.

Barring extenuating circumstances, the answer was ten years.

All right then. Let's see what was going on in this little town ten years ago.

CHAPTER 18

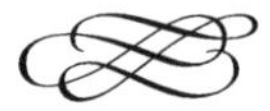

It was seven o'clock. I searched for the closing time for the Brookfield's library and saw I had another hour. I needed to hurry to make it.

I shoved one last fry in my mouth then reached for my wallet. I left a twenty under the plate and grabbed my stuff.

Several of the retired men at the counter told me to have a good night on my way out. Made me smile.

About two seconds later the smile got wiped right off my face. I ran into Sharon, Jan's cousin and the beautician from A Cut Above. She had several friends with her and they were talking as fast as a gaggle of hens, all with the same bouffant hairstyle.

She stopped dead in her tracks when she saw me. "Well, honey! What have you done with your hair?"

"Oh, I've just been working all day," I said, brushing it behind my ear.

"I see." She nodded. "Well, maybe don't tell anyone I cut it unless it's styled, okay?"

I nodded, dumbly, suddenly feeling like a sheep dog.

"You have a good night!" she said cheerfully, unaware of the karate chop she'd just given my confidence.

Well, who is she anyway? My haircut alone was bad for her business. Huffing a little, I got into my car. I was fuming and it took me three typos before I was able to punch the library into my GPS. As it searched, I yanked down the visor and peered into the mirror.

I look okay. What's she talking about?

I flipped the visor back with a snap and started the car. A streetlight flickered until it blinked off as I drove under it. It reminded me of my dad. I smiled, thinking of how he believed it was his personal electromagnetic charge swirling in his body that caused lights to do that. I never had the heart to break it to him that I'd heard they were on timers. He was happy thinking it was his superpower.

The GPS led me down the street a few blocks and then directed me to turn. Over here was the more quiet side of the town. The streets were lined with old fashioned balloon lights, which added to the charm.

I pulled into the library parking lot and parked.

I was lucky I made it all the way in the stall, because I'd just caught a glimpse of something that made me suck in a breath.

Standing in front of the door was a bronze statue of a mom bringing her daughter inside.

I sat frozen, my hands locked into two claws on my seatbelt. Unannounced, and frankly unwanted, tears stung my eyes as a memory replayed of my mom taking me to a library very similar to this one.

It had been at Christmas time and the library was putting on a puppet show of the Nutcracker. I don't know how old I was, I must have been under five. I remember squealing when they flashed the lights for the angry mouse's appearance. Mom had scooped me up on her lap and I'd finished watching from the safety of her arms.

A tear trickled down my cheek. I sniffed and wiped it away. It was odd. Her face was a blur of dark hair and a smile, but her scent. I could remember that like it was yesterday. She'd used Baby Soft cologne. Even now, when I caught the scent of baby powder, it would be enough to remind me of her.

And then she left. Dad never told me why.

One day, I'd find out. I promised myself.

I took in a deep breath and blew it out. *Okay, Focus. Let's just go inside and see if your hunch is reliable or not.*

The darkness was welcome as I got out of the car, allowing me to hide my vulnerability. I took a few cleansing breaths. Feeling stronger, I walked up to the entrance and patted the bronze girl's head on the way to the door. I was glad I'd seen it, now that I had time to process that flash of memory. It was a reminder that I didn't need to squash the good memories, trying to protect myself. I saw my dad doing that, and it still made me feel sad.

My hand was on the door when I noticed there was a book drop that opened into the building. A large sign next to it said, "When you drop in a book, please holler, 'Not a squirrel!'"

What in the...? I chuckled. I needed the story behind this.

I opened the door and walked inside to be immediately wrapped in the lovely scent of books, the quiet hush of pages turning, and the click of computer keys. I was surprised to see so many patrons here at this time of night. Made me wonder if people read more in small towns because there wasn't a lot else to do.

The librarian was over by the long check-out desk,

rearranging books on a metal cart. She seemed extremely focused as she muttered to herself.

I walked over and waited quietly, but she never looked up. After a moment, I said, "Can I bother you? I'm not a squirrel."

The librarian glanced up with surprise. Her glasses were askew and her face flushed. She nudged her glasses in place. "Oh, were you standing there long? Sorry, we just had a huge inventory come in from the holds." She smiled. "So how can I help you, Not-a-squirrel?"

I pointed to the front doors. "I have to know what that's about. Are there a lot of squirrel readers?"

She laughed. "We have several beech trees out front. You'd be surprised how many of those varmints try to get through that flap to hide their nuts. We've tried everything to deter them. Now, whenever we hear rattling, one of us runs over with a net if the noise goes on too long."

The image of librarians flying around with nets, chasing squirrels made me chuckle. "That's hilarious. Well, while I have you, I'm trying to find some newspaper records for the last ten years."

"Oh, sure. You just head to the back where you'll see a microfilm catalogue. It's as ancient as the hills, but it gets the job done."

"Thank you," I said and left her to sort out the stack of books.

I was embarrassed to admit how much time had passed since I'd actually been in a library, but the layout was the same. There were the expected long shelves of books, each row labeled with a genre, and scattered stools and chairs.

I walked past a row of tables, each lit with a desk lamp. Some had computer monitors and some were bare. In the darkest corner of the building, I found the cabinet she'd referred to.

Okay, where to start. I slid open a drawer and scanned the folders. The microfilms were organized by topics. I quickly found the Brookfield Gazette and flipped through years.

Starting at a decade ago, I slid a microfilm out of the plastic envelope and put it under the light of the viewer. I spun the dial to get it to focus. Slowly, I pushed the film to scan it on the screen.

There was news on the stock trades, news of our troops overseas, store announcements of openings and closings, gas prices, and grocery store sales. There were also lots of weddings, funerals, and birth announcements.

But I didn't see one article for a missing person. I grabbed another at nine years ago and scrolled. Still nothing. I continued until I was at just five years ago. I wasn't comfortable going any closer. I didn't think a body would be reduced to a skeleton any sooner.

Nothing.

Now I began checking the years after the ten-year mark. I have to admit, I was starting to get that tight, frustrated sensation in my guts. Maybe I needed to expand my search for the entire county, rather than just this one town's newspaper.

Then, something popped up on the twelfth year. There'd been a big crime that happened in the county and headlines about it showed up again and again throughout that year.

Two police officers had been shot during an attempted bank robbery.

Curious, I zoomed in on one of the articles. **Police No Closer to Solving the Robbery.**

I read through the story. It said that one officer had been injured with shots fired as the suspect ran away. One thing that stuck out was that it was at a jewelry store. I remembered the shiny watch on the skeleton's arm. Was that just some weird coincidence? Still, I took note of the officers' names who were involved in it that day. Maybe I could track them down to ask a few questions.

Funny how, being that my grandfather was a former FBI agent, I was getting into this detective gig ever since I moved back to Pennsylvania. Maybe it was in my blood, after all.

CHAPTER 19

The drive home was uneventful but that's not what my fresh paranoia led me to believe. Every time a car pulled out behind me, I stared into the rearview mirror, searching for those perfectly round headlights.

Back at the house, I brought in my bags of clothes and purse and dumped them all on the counter. I'd deal with this mess tomorrow. Right now, I wanted to do a search to see where those police officers were now.

It turned out, the first one had retired, which was no surprise given his age. I was pretty happy to see that the second was still working at the Brookfield police force.

There was a recent picture of the police officer, which I quickly zoomed in. He had to be close to retiring, as well. His face had more wrinkles than a silk scarf that'd been accidentally washed. By comparison, his shock of hair was surprisingly thick and black. Was it hair dye? A toupee? I jotted down the police department's number. I'd call tomorrow and see if he was available to talk. At least I could ask if a watch had been among the stolen goods.

But if the skeleton was the robber, why would he break into the Valentine's house? There were hundreds of houses closer. Heck, if you were shot and bleeding, was it even possible to break into a room on the third story? This just didn't make any sense.

Still, it was all I had.

Sighing, I pushed away from the computer and got into my pajamas. It'd been a long day. I grabbed my great-great-grandmother's stack of letters and climbed into bed with my notepad. After flipping on the table lamp, I snuggled into the pillows and opened another letter, before finding my translate app on my phone. Lots of henpecking, squinting and guessing ensued after that. It took a lot of deciphering but in the end, this is what I had.

My Dearest Mother,

I've made the arduous journey to Ellis Island. There were many times I did not think I would escape Poland. Our sweet land. I was given food by farmers several times. Once, I hid in a haystack outside of Krakow when the troops made their search. I could hear them march by and I was terrified they would question the farmers. I was able to get passage on the Wojtek. The trip on the ship was long, but I'm here and safe. I wait for you to join me.

Your loving daughter,

Wiktoria

I had chills as I read it. Grandma Wiktoria, I'm figuring you out. You were incredible!

Yawning, I placed the stuff on the table and flipped the light off. I pulled up the blankets and stared up at the ceiling. I was still smiling.

The next morning, I called the police station. Amazingly, I was able to set up a meeting with the officer later that day. I picked up the lucky charm from the kitchen counter and flipped the squirrel in my hand. I was ready for some answers.

That day was fairly slow at Flamingo Realty, with Kari mostly chasing down a few leads from the open house the day before. She let me leave early with a wave of her hand, the phone pressed against her ear.

I drove to the sheriff's office which, coincidentally, was right behind the Darcy's Doughnuts that Kari had met me at earlier in the week.

It took me a minute to find parking since all of the available spots were filled with police cars. Finally, after finding one about half-way up the block, I walked back to the building. Two officers were leaving as I entered, and one held the door open for me.

Okay. Here it goes. I walked up to the front desk. There a very tired and harried looking woman sat in a visibly broken chair. She was sorting through a plastic filing cabinet. It was hard to miss the fact that the back of the chair was swathed in duct tape.

She must have heard me come in. Her chair squeaked loudly as she turned to face me. "Can I help you?"

"Hi. I have an appointment with Officer Benson?"

She glanced at her planner and nodded. "Go down the hall. His is the first desk on the left."

"Thank you," I said, but before I even had the words out, she had already returned to her task.

I walked down the hall. It was freezing in the building and felt like the thermostat hadn't been touched since last year. I crossed my arms and peeked into the main room.

It was filled with desks, not sitting in neat rows, but

haphazard as if scattered by giant children who were done with their play. Each desk had a pair of metal folding chairs in front of it. Most of the desks were empty, but a few had officers sitting in front of their computers.

There was a large man at the second one. I recognized him from the photo last night.

He looked up as I walked over.

"Officer Benson?" I asked.

"Oh, you must be my three o'clock. Miss...?"

"Stella O'Neil," I said. I wasn't sure if I should shake and thrust out my hand anyway.

He ignored it, shuffling through a stack of papers instead. I brought it back, caught a little off guard.

"Please, have a seat." He indicated one of the chairs with a raise of his bushy eyebrows, still not looking up.

I pulled it out and sat, immediately gritting my teeth from the cold metal. I pressed my hands together between my knees and squeezed to keep from shivering.

"Thank you for meeting me, Officer Benson," I said, glancing around.

It was a little weird to be back here. I knew cops had work spaces but I'd never actually been in one before. I mean here it was, a desk, with a cop staring at me from across it. I giggled inside, so wanting to snap a picture and send it to my dad with the words, "Help!"

Officer Benson finished sorting his papers and leaned back in his chair. "What can I do for you, Miss O'Neil?"

"I ran across a robbery that happened twelve years ago."

He pressed his lips together and exhaled heavily. "Mmhmm."

"It was a jewelry store burglary that went wrong."

"I see. What brought questions about this case about?"

"So, I don't know if you heard, but I'm the realtor, or at least the assistant, to a house for sale up in old town. The Valentine Manor?"

He folded his hands and rested them on his desk. He didn't say anything but I could tell by the way he was studying me that he was interested.

My throat suddenly felt dry. I cleared it, and then coughed.

"Would you like some water?" he asked.

I nodded and he got up heavily. He lumbered over to a water fountain and filled a plastic cup. This he brought back and set in front of me.

I sipped it gratefully. "Thank you," I said.

"You were saying?"

"I was doing some research and came across that crime. Did that person ever get caught? The one that got away?"

"Get caught?" He smirked at me. I wasn't sure why, so I tried to clarify.

"Yeah, get caught. Like did he rob another jewelry store? Or did you find out who he was through video footage?"

"Camera footage wasn't nearly as widely used as it is now, despite all those cop shows you might have seen on TV. We didn't have dash cameras and body cams. Especially out here in these parts." He rubbed the side of his nose. "We did however, lift a picture from the jewelry store surveillance." He turned to his computer and started typing. After a minute, he spun the screen around to me.

A grainy, black-and-white photo of a man stared directly at the camera. He wasn't young, like I expected. More like a man in his late forties. I was surprised at his age. I stared harder. He seemed vaguely familiar, in a weird way.

I looked back at Officer Benson. "Did you see him, personally? I mean, I know he shot at you guys."

Suddenly, I blushed, realizing how stupid and insensitive I sounded. "Are you okay? Did it heal up?"

"Yeah, I healed up pretty well. You were asking if I caught

him. Well, we did something that we thought would catch him, but it never panned out."

"What do you mean?" I asked.

"We never released this information, but we were scouting the hospitals afterward. You see, Miss O'Neil. He didn't just shoot us. I got him too."

"You shot him?" I asked.

"Yeah. I did. He was running away, but it hit him in the leg."

I raised my eyebrows.

"He should have showed up at a hospital. We searched everywhere in all the state's counties but no one showed up."

"What about like vet clinics?"

He snorted again. "You do watch a lot of movies, don't you?"

"Well, I don't know?" I answered, lamely.

"Vets don't generally work on people without alerting us."

"Maybe he took care of it himself."

"Like with Grandma's sewing kit?"

I was digging myself in deeper. The one thing I hated was to appear foolish, and I was edging dangerously close to that territory.

"Not a sewing kit, exactly," I said. "But you know..."

"Poke the bullet out with a knife, douse it with alcohol and sew it up. Or maybe super glue it? That's the newest rage, right?"

I kept quiet. Was I being ridiculous or was he being smug? I couldn't tell.

He must have realized how he was coming across because his smile softened. "Aw, I'm sorry. I'm yanking your chain. You don't deserve it. Seriously, I hit him with a nine mm and there ain't no way he was going to be able to dig that one out at home."

"So, what do you think happened to him?"

"I think he either has connections we don't know about, or he ended up holed somewhere for a few days."

"What if I have an idea where he holed up?"

"You think you can solve that cold case?"

I shrugged. "What about the skeleton discovered at the Valentine's?"

"Listen, you want me to dig into that, you need to show me a connection between the robber and the Valentines. Right now I don't have the time to track down every unidentified body that's found to see if it's from a burglary twelve years ago. But I'll look into this, if you promise to see what you can learn on your end."

My confusion still ensued. He rolled his eyes, obviously done with me. "Just tell me what the Valentine's are saying about the skeleton. Keep me in the loop." With that, he heaved his considerable bulk from the chair. "Now, if you don't mind, I have an interrogation in room two."

"Of course," I said, standing as well. I followed him out to the hall, where he went to the left and I went to the right. I waved goodbye to the receptionist, who barely glanced up as I left.

CHAPTER 20

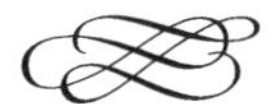

How in the world was I going to find a connection between the burglar and the Valentines?

I sat in my car, my head against the backrest. Two steps forward, one step back, I swear.

All right. I've got to move forward. What can I do from here?

I needed to find some more information about the Valentines. Surely they weren't as mysterious as they seemed. Everyone has a past, after all. The microfilm at the library came to mind, and I decided it deserved a revisit.

Parking at the library this time wasn't nearly so dramatic. It's true, the bronze statue gave my heart another squeeze, but it didn't evoke the tears of last time. I hurried in and found my way back to the same cabinets as yesterday.

All right, little Brookfield Gazette. Give me all you've got. I yanked open the cabinet and pushed through the film to the way back. I figured I needed to start around the 1930's if I wanted to find birth announcements for their family.

The clock ticked in the background as I studied the microfilm. I started out enchanted at the old time news and ads. Look at the quaint medicines! But, as more and more time passed, I ignored everything except the word Valentine.

After a few more minutes—and a tiny giggle of triumph—I found the birth announcement for Gladys. She was a baby like the rest of us, diapers and all! I smiled bigger, thinking how she'd hate to be thought of that way.

The announcement was formal and flowery, with all the basic information you'd expect. I read it feeling like I won the lottery. In fact, my cheeks hurt from grinning.

After a bit more time, I also tracked down the announcements for both Charity, and Richard.

Everything was to be as expected. Except for one thing.

I couldn't find anything for the baby.

That was beyond bizarre. I knew there'd been an infant. I'd seen the picture. Frustrated, I continued my search, paragraphs and frames of the film flashing on the screen. There was a birth announcement for Marla Springfield, from the Springfield restaurant which caught my attention, but nothing for the last Valentine baby.

I rubbed my forehead, where pressure building warned of a coming stress headache. I couldn't believe it. I flipped forward a year , still nothing. Flipped to the next year. Nothing.

A tingling sensation twirled in my stomach. Something was up. To be thorough, I checked clear through the next twenty years. There were no more Valentine birth announcements.

I was about to give up when I found something else quite intriguing. Gladys's formal ball. The announcement declared it was held at their house, and in the snobbish tone, it pontificated that all of Brookfield's elite attended.

Well, la-di-da. I zoomed in on the picture. Framed in a dark background was a beautifully dressed Ms. Valentine with a quiet Mona Lisa's smile so similar to her mom's. Surrounding her were several young men dressed to the hilt. The photo had these words under it.

Brookfield's most eligible bachelors take turns swinging a blushing Miss Valentine out on the dance floor.

I sat back in the library chair and blinked. With all of those eligible men, why hadn't Gladys Valentine ever married? It seemed to me that back then there was a rush to get married, with the title "old maid" applied to single woman who—by today's standards—were still quite young.

It was hard for me to coincide the grumpy woman I knew now to the fresh-faced woman in the photo. She'd been so pretty. Her family quite rich. That sounded to me like all the right ingredients for men from miles around to come wooing. What on earth happened?

Come to think of it, Charity hadn't married, either. My eyebrows flew up in shock. Nor Richard! How weird that all three—maybe four since I still hadn't found any information on the baby—of the children had remained single.

Something *had* to have happened. I rubbed my temple again. It seemed the rabbit hole of the Valentine family was deeper than I realized.

Leaning forward, I scrolled through the end of the year. There was a wedding announcement for Marla Springfield and Kyle Murphy. My jaw dropped. Was *that* the Valentine's Kyle? It had to be. The infamous Kyle...wow. Why hadn't Marla mentioned the name of her husband when we talked at the restaurant?

The article listed the rest of the wedding party. I paused when I came to the maid of honor's name; Gladys Valentine.

Well now. What have we here? Marla had said she'd had a

falling out with Gladys. In fact, she said all of the Valentines had quit talking to her.

I kept scrolling. Later that month was an announcement congratulating the heroes who were leaving for Korea. Among those on the list were Richard Valentine and Kyle Murphy.

I was right. Marla *had* been married to that Kyle.

I remembered she said she filed for divorce while her husband was in Korea.

Last among the announcements was a notice of death for Elisabeth Valentine. I assumed that must have been Mrs. Valentine when I saw that she was survived by her children, Gladys, Charity and Richard, along with her husband.

Weird and weirder. There was no mention of a fourth child.

Who was that baby? There was no birth announcement and no death announcement for anyone else in the Valentine family.

I grabbed a pen and started doodling a list. Okay, what did I know about Kyle?

He was taken in by the Valentine's because their father felt pity for him when his family died, but he turned out to be quite the mess.

He married Marla later and then she divorced him.

She called him a cheater.

Mrs. Crawford was still in touch with him.

I stared at the list as more pieces started tumbling around. Most notably, the fact that Marla and Gladys had a falling out in their friendship. I knew they had once been close, as evidenced by Gladys being in Marla's wedding.

I gasped. I knew what had happened, and I knew who the baby was. Of course! Gladys must have had an affair with Kyle.

Which meant the baby was the son of Gladys Valentine and Kyle Murphy.

Back in the 50's, having a child out of wedlock was a huge taboo. Families even sent their daughters away so that no one would know. As an elite family in the town, it would have been a secret the Valentines never would have wanted out. Especially since the baby had come from an affair. They would have been black listed from everything. They would have been ruined.

I remembered the scripture that had been highlighted with the picture of the baby. It had mentioned, "In sin did my mother conceive me."

I guess that the original Mrs. Valentine must have tried to

pass the baby off as hers. But when she died, the baby disappeared as well. Where did he go?

So far, I've found skeleton's left and right in the Valentine family line, like people had warned me. But they weren't helping me on identifying the real skeleton that I'd found in the bedroom.

I figured I'd email Officer Benson with what I learned, although at this point it felt more like gossip you'd hear at the local beauty parlor. Which made me think of Jan from the Post Office. Maybe I should visit her one more time. After all, I remembered how she liked to talk. Maybe if I came with some direct questions, she'd have something more to say.

I glanced at the clock and saw it was about fifteen minutes before five. Without another thought, I grabbed my purse and headed out of the library.

My brain spun my newly-learned facts around as I drove, like all those details were socks in the washing machine. I hoped Jan was working. It was nearly five when I found a parking spot right in front of the post office and squeezed my car in, then jumped out. I ran for the door just as Jan was coming with the keys.

"Hi!" I said breathlessly. "Is there any way I can get a book of stamps before you close?" Wow, I was becoming an expert at popping off these excuses.

She glanced at her watch, her dutch-boy haircut falling forward. "Sure, we have about five minutes. It's been a slow as molasses kind of day so I was just going to flip the sign. But we still have time."

Jan led me to the back. Her sensible shoes scraped against the linoleum. Squeak. Squeak. Squeak. I didn't know how she could stand that noise all day. She went to her drawer and pulled out several books from a drawer and set them on the counter. "How many you need?" Her eyebrows raised with a look that said she'd seen people buy a plethora of stamps and nothing could surprise her.

"Oh," I scrambled in my purse for my wallet. "One is fine."

She sighed as she slid the unwanted books away. "So, how's it going up at the Valentine Manor?" Her tone was casual and she looked through a pile of junk mail as if to highlight how uninterested she was.

I bit back a smile. So she wanted to do a little fishing for info, as well. That was good for me.

"It's been okay." I hesitated a second, before blurting, "I saw a couple pictures. One of Kyle and Richard in their uniforms."

"Mm." She nodded. "Those two were trouble personified."

"Really?" I asked, grabbing my stamps as an excuse to lean closer.

"Oh, you betcha. They were what we called Greasers back in the day. You have any idea what they were? Troublemakers for sure. Quite the little thieves."

"Thieves, huh? Did they ever get caught?"

"Why do you think Mr. Valentine was in such a rush to get them into the military?"

"Sounds like they really did everything together. I bet you're surprised Kyle never came back to see Richard. Has he ever been back?"

"They had a falling out," Jan said. "Honestly, it's no surprise. Kyle Murphy wasn't ever close to anyone. Not even with his parents before they died. And then, when Marla divorced him, I suppose he didn't have a reason to return."

"Speaking of the family, I saw a picture of all of the Valentines together." I hesitated, not sure how I was going to explain what I saw in the picture. "Interestingly, besides the three kids there was a baby as well."

Her expression of interest dropped like a curtain. Suddenly, she seemed done with this conversation. "You be careful what that tells you right there."

"Tell me what?" I asked. This was what I was waiting for.

She pushed back my debit card. "Anything else?"

"No, no that's all." I tried again with new bait. "Did you ever think it was weird that none of them have kids?"

"How do you know that?"

"Well, I mean..." I shrugged. Wasn't it obvious? "None of the Valentine's are married."

"Honey, you don't have to be married to have a baby."

Oh, she was hovering over the hook! "But they seem so proper," I teased out.

She shrugged. "There are rumors. Lots of rumors. I'm surprised you haven't heard of them yet."

This is what I was waiting for. I leaned in closer and tried to keep the look of eagerness from my face like I was a cat about to pounce on the canary. "What kinds of rumors?"

"Juicy ones. Ones you should know if you're selling that house."

"Juicy, like how?"

Jan shrugged. "Let's just say, if there was a baby, maybe the baby disappeared right around the time Kyle did."

"Was Gladys the mom?" I whispered.

The bell above the door rang.

She glanced behind me and straightened. "Will there be anything else?"

I glanced behind me and saw a woman at the counter filling out a form. It looked like it would take her a minute. Surely Jan had time to answer my question? I looked back to see a stiff smile on Jan's face. I was dismissed, no doubt about it.

What was it about this town keeping the Valentine's secrets?

CHAPTER 21

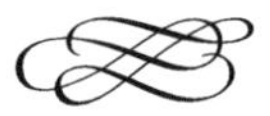

"I have great news!" Kari squealed through the phone. "We have a buyer for the Valentine mansion!"

"That *is* great!" Was she serious! This house really was about to be in my rearview mirror after all!

"Well, the only problem is that I am completely booked for today. Do you feel comfortable enough to swing by the place and get the family to sign it? It's completely cut and dried. The buyers didn't ask for anything out of the contract. And when the Valentines have finished, put up the sale pending sign?"

I'd covered that aspect in my online realty class, and was beginning to get the feeling that Kari liked having an assistant. "Absolutely, I can do it. I guess you can just text me the details and..."

"Awesome, thanks! Everything you need will be on my desk." And then there was a dial tone.

Okay, then.

Of course, it would happen right now. The movers had called and were finally showing up with my things this afternoon.

I was looking forward to my full wardrobe. I pulled the second outfit out of the bag that I'd bought the other day and got ready to go.

Tan slacks, a pastel pink camisole, and a cup of coffee in my hand later, I was out the door. I drove straight to the Flamingo Realty. No one was there, but Uncle Chris had given me the key. I walked inside and over to Kari's desk where I found everything as expected. I glanced over the forms and saw that the buyer was a company called Diamond Enterprises. I typed the name into my browser on my phone, which came up with a site that said they provided "luxury condominiums and vacation rentals."

I raised my eyebrows. It seemed like the small town's fears of getting more traffic in the future were true.

I grabbed the stuff and headed back to my car, being sure to lock the door on my way out.

As I drove, I saw a grandpa walking into a restaurant with his grandson. It reminded me, when was I going to work up the guts to see Oscar? He was half the reason I moved out here. How many more times was I going to drive past his place?

Soon, I promised myself. *When I get this Valentine business wrapped up.*

I glanced at the Sold sign bouncing on the seat next to me as I rattled down the road. Soon was coming up awfully fast.

I pulled into the Valentine driveway and parked the car. I smiled, so excited to nearly be done with this place. As I walked up to the porch, I saw the carved heart I'd seen before, the one that was scratched out. I leaned down to see if I could make it out any better.

There was definitely a K, which could stand for Kyle. But what was the other initial? Despite being scraped, there was an odd flourish still visible that seemed strange to be a part of a G for Gladys. I puzzled over it, wondering what it was.

The door opened then, making me jerk up.

"Ms. O'Neil," Ms. Valentine said. She smiled. "Ms. Missler said you'd be stopping by with an offer."

Her brother, Richard, popped up behind her. "She's probably going to try and get us to accept something that will rob us blind."

"Now, Richard. Ms. O'Neil is quite capable. I'm sure she has our best interests in mind."

My mouth dropped. Was Ms. Valentine being the voice of kindness?

Was a certain fiery place freezing over?

"Hello. Yes. I do have some papers to go over with you." I fumbled the folder of papers, managing to drop the pen. I picked up the pen and dropped the sold sign. When I glanced up, Richard had disappeared. Ms. Valentine stared down her nose in her usual disapproving way.

"I don't happen to have much faith in your competence, but it's important to make a show of confidence in front of my siblings. I hope you won't make me regret my support."

I grinned—a bitter one—and stared right back. I'd had just about enough. I'd cleaned this house, stayed all weekend to show potential buyers, talked to police, and overcame my fears just so that I could help sell her manor.

I could feel it bubbling up— a low blow. It was coming. I gritted my jaw to stop it.

"Are you coming in, or are you here to waste my time again?" she asked.

"I noticed this carving here," I said, lightly touching it.

Her eyes went wide as she glanced at it.

"It looks like a K and a G. Was that you and Kyle?"

Her mouth opened even wider than her eyes. I immediately kicked myself. I thought for sure she was going to slam the door in my face, but instead she brought her cane around front and leaned on it with both hands.

She raised her eyebrows. "I knew you were snooping. What have you seen?"

Well, score one for her. I wasn't expecting to be confronted so boldly. But it was true. I *had* been snooping. And for good reason. I'd found a dead person in her house.

I lifted my chin and answered, "I saw a picture of your family. There was a baby in it, a baby that no one acknowledges or seems to have any information about. Was that baby yours and Kyle Murphy's?"

Her eyes hardened as she watched me. Her gaze chilled me, like she could see something inside me that I didn't know myself. I shifted slightly.

"You think I'm Kyle's illicit lover?"

I licked my lip and nodded. "I think that was a good possibility. Is that why Marla cut her friendship off from you?"

"Well, you're wrong. Dead wrong." She laughed then, shocking me to my core. Her eye sparkled with a superiority as though I were ridiculous with my conjecture.

I didn't know how to recover, to be honest. I stood there, like a catfish that had just been caught by noodling, papers limp in my hand, wondering what to do next. Do I just carry on like nothing had happened?

Ms. Valentine knew she'd won that round. "Now, are you ready to come in, or shall we continue?"

I swallowed and lifted the folder. "Time to sign, I think," I said.

She led me down the hall, her cane making its characteristic thumping. There was a moment she veered toward the library and I panicked, but then she opened the study door.

"Charity! Richard!" she called.

I went over the offer as quickly as possible like my realty classes had taught me. There was nothing unexpected, which is probably why Kari allowed me to do it. Richard signed and then immediately left. I heard the car gun it outside, and dirt spit as he drove away.

Ms. Valentine—spurning my offered pen and using her old-fashioned metal nub ink pen, carefully signed her name.

It was as Charity was signing that I noticed a flourish she

used on the C. Very similar to the one carved into the pole outside.

I glanced up at Ms. Valentine, and she narrowed her eyes.

I gulped and looked back down. *Don't say anything. Just get these things signed.*

They finished signing and I gathered the papers up. No one spoke. Honestly, I left the house with a flood of relief. *Shake the dust off your feet,* I thought as I walked down the steps.

As I walked to my car, I noticed a pick-up truck out at the end of the driveway. The back had a weed-eater poking out. Maybe they were a local yard worker looking for new clients.

As I reached my car, my gaze landed on the shed in the back, and I remembered when I'd seen someone there. And, just like last time, I saw movement at the small building. Pausing, I held my breath, hoping it would be Richard poking around. The figure began to walk from behind the building but saw me and jumped back. My heart sped up.

He wasn't tall enough to be Richard.

I looked around but there was no one around to help. It was up to me.

"Hello? Can I help you?" I asked, slowly walking toward the shed and hoping I wasn't being the dumb girl in the horror movies that you scream at for going toward the danger.

There was a crash in the building.

"Hey! I'm calling the police!" I pulled out my phone when the man came running around the side and toward me.

"Wait, wait!" He held his hands up in front of himself, showing me they were empty. "Please don't do that! I'm not going to hurt you."

Hurt me? I pressed the 9 and the 1. "Who are you?" I held my phone in front of me, my finger waiting to push the last 1.

As he got closer, I saw he was quite old. He walked with a limp.

"Please, I just..." He rubbed his hands through his gray hair, sighing. "Look, I know this family and this house."

I wasn't sure what to say. "You need to go up to the front door then and knock. Why are you wandering around back there?"

"I'm sorry," he said.

"Who are you?" I repeated.

He ignored me and reached into his back pocket, causing me to hold up the phone, finger poised. "Watch it!" I yelled.

He held out a hand. In the other one was a newspaper. "They found a skeleton here. Do they know who it is?"

I stood, shocked and unsure of what to do next. Where the

heck was Richard? He was always skulking about. Ms. Valentine? Charity?

The man stared at me with dark eyes. He was watching me, trying to read what I was thinking.

That expression reminded me of someone.

I swallowed and asked, "How do you know the Valentines?"

"Mr. Valentine was a caring man. I messed up, okay? He took me in like one of his own but...no, I'm not a Valentine. But my son was."

"Your son?" I could barely hear him through the rushing of blood in my ears.

"Yes. Charity's and my son."

My mouth dropped. His eyes watched me, his empty hand still loose and non-threatening, but something had my body in the fight or flight mode.

I picked up my jaw enough to ask, "Kyle Murphy?"

He didn't answer, but he didn't deny it. "I just want to see Charity. I have some questions. Is there any way you can get me in?"

My determination rose quickly. "No, there's no way I can just let you in. I mean, let me get...Gladys."

"No!" Anger colored his face red. "No! I don't want her or Richard knowing I'm here. They've always hated me. All these years. There's no way they'd let me see her."

"Why not?" I shot a look toward the windows, wondering if anyone had seen us yet. Maybe they would call the cops or come out and save me all the trouble and panic.

"It's a long story, I just want to see Charity and talk to her for just a minute, okay? I want to ask her about this."

He still held the newspaper in his hand.

"What questions do you have for her? Who do you think the skeleton is?" I asked. I was scared to hear the answer.

CHAPTER 22

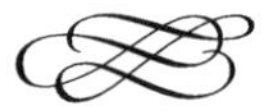

"Who was it?" I asked again, my voice ratcheting up with anxiety.

"I think it was Brian. My son. Charity's and my son."

"How?" I asked, reeling at hearing what I'd suspected to be true coming from his mouth.

"He'd been shot in the leg. It was serious, but not deadly. I don't know why he didn't make it." Kyle stared at me beseechingly, almost begging for understanding. "I'm not a monster. I'm not a good man, either, but I didn't leave him alone to die. I should have protected him."

"How did he get shot?" I felt sick to my stomach. I knew, but I wanted to hear him say it.

"He was just like his old man, always in trouble. Only he never outgrew it." Kyle glanced at the newspaper article and his face crumpled as his eyes filled with tears. "Honestly, I wasn't the best man, but I tried. I really tried with him. After Mrs. Valentine died, Gladys forced Brian into my arms and told me I had to take him. That Charity was fragile and couldn't handle the stigma of having a baby out of wedlock. No one knew it was hers. No one does to this day."

He lifted his head. His eyes were red-rimmed. "I moved him clear to Ohio to try to give the boy a new beginning. I gave it my best shot. But, it was drugs that got that boy, and once they grabbed hold, they never let go. Then, he found out that I'd been writing a woman here."

"Do you mean Mrs. Crawford?"

He started with surprise and then gave a hollow laugh. "You know about her, too? Yeah, it wasn't too hard for Brian to get the whole story out of me. Well, he thought he could come back to the Valentine Manor and force them to accept him. It didn't work out so well. I don't even know if he got to say who he was before Gladys had Richard toss him out on his ear. Brian called me. I could hear the shaking in his voice, and thought it was from drugs."

A tear ran down Kyle's cheek. "He said he'd gotten into trouble. That he'd been shot in the leg. I'm still not sure what happened. He said I needed to come and he'd be waiting for me down in the woods behind the town's park. I told Brian to call an ambulance, but he said he needed me."

He sighed. "I jumped in the car immediately, but it was still a five hour drive. On my way, I called Gladys to see if she'd help him. I told her where Brian was, begged her to help him. 'He's your blood!' I reminded her. She hung up on me. When I went to the spot that Brian said he'd be at, he wasn't there. I spent the next two weeks searching for him."

"Did you come here, too?" I asked, gesturing toward the house.

"Yeah, it was the first place I came. I was hoping that Gladys had relented. That somewhere in her cold heart, she'd felt a drop of mercy and had come to that boy's aid. Her nephew. But she denied it. Said she'd never seen him, and then Richard came out with his gun and told me to leave."

My heart ached to see his pain. At the same time, his words scared me. "You think Brian made it here after all."

Kyle didn't say anything. Just crumpled the paper and nodded.

I vaguely heard the rev of an engine, but it didn't register, amidst the horrible truth that was implied by Kyle's nod. I glanced down, suddenly drowning in my own thoughts.

A sudden weight slammed into my waist as Kyle knocked me to the ground.

I beat at Kyle with my hands until I realized the old Valentine car skidded to a stop exactly where we'd both been standing.

If he hadn't knocked me to the ground I would have been hit. I could have been killed.

Fury filled me and I started to scream to give the driver a piece of my mind. All stopped when the car door sprang open. Richard got out with a shotgun in his hands.

I gasped, feeling like I'd been punched in the gut. I didn't have air to defend myself, or breath to plead.

He pulled back the lever, his face dark with anger. He leveled it at me, and I swear the whole world started to swim.

Then I realized he was pointing the rifle at Kyle.

"It's over now, boy," Richard said, his voice shaking with fury.

Think, Stella.

I glanced down at my hand and sent up a quick thank you as I saw I still held my phone. I pushed the last 1 on the cell, completing the emergency call. Now my hope was that police would respond faster than Richard could decide to shoot Kyle.

"Richard, we can figure this out. I have an answer," I bluffed, holding my hand up in a way that I hoped was calming.

He didn't even look at me.

"Noooooo!" A blood-curdling shriek came from behind us.

I was too afraid to look away from the gun to see who was screaming. I didn't normally play hero, but I hoped by staring Richard in the eye, he'd be less likely to shoot.

Charity leaped into the tangled pile of us on the ground. She wrapped her arms around Kyle. I was astounded at the strength and speed of the short woman.

"Richard, no!" she cried, holding tightly to Kyle. Kyle said nothing. In fact, he hadn't even moved.

"Get out of the way, Charity," Richard growled.

We stared back like three owls at Richard.

Richard's jaw jumped as he chewed his cheek. Slowly, he lowered his gun. But he wasn't done yet. "I said, get away from him!"

I shimmied backward to get clear of them, before glancing at my phone. It was connected to the police. I could hear the faint voice repeatedly asking if I was there.

I lifted it to my ear and whispered, hoping I wouldn't distract

Richard. "Yes, I'm at the Valentine mansion! Please send help."

"Where?"

I rattled off the address I knew by heart now.

"What's the nature of the emergency?"

"There's a man with a gun and I don't know if he is going to shoot someone or not."

"Where is the gunman? Has he shot anyone?"

"No, he's just really mad and he was pointing it at another man but his sister stopped him."

"How did she stop him?"

The questions were infuriating. "She's blocking his shot. Please hurry!"

Meanwhile, Charity was talking animatedly to Richard. Frowning, her brother slowly raised his shotgun again.

"Stop, Richard! The police are on their way!" I walked over with my hands in the air until I was standing in front of the two that stayed on the ground. What was I doing?

I was trying to save someone's life, that's what I was doing.

"What's going on here?" An abrupt question jerked our attention to the side. Gladys strode forward, her cane stabbing into the ground and pulling out divots. Her eyes passed over me and locked onto Richard.

"What are you doing?" she asked her brother, before drawing her gaze down to Charity and Kyle.

"Charity, what is the meaning of...." she trailed off when she saw who Charity was protecting. Her lips pressed into a grim line.

I tensed, my arms still out, like a cat about to spring away.

"Richard, put the gun away now. The police are on their way, unless Ms. O'Neil would care to stop that." She glared at me.

The answer was a hard no from me. How did I know what was going to happen next?

"Ms. Valentine, they already know about a gun..."

"Lovely. Well, everyone needs to get out of the yard and come inside, at the very least. The neighbors surely have gossip for years to come already and once the police arrive, we'll have a crowd." She reached down and grabbed Kyle's shoulder. "Inside, now. Everyone. Richard, you too."

Kyle patted Charity on the arm and whispered to her. She smiled at him, her face glowing, and allowed him to help her stand.

This place really was the funny farm. I glanced at my car, overcome with desire to race away.

Two things stopped me, I knew the cops would want to know where I was when they arrived. I did call them, after all. And I wasn't so sure about Kyle's safety if I did leave.

We all slowly moved into the parlor. Kyle sat in one chair, and Charity in another. Richard stood by the fireplace and Ms. Valentine sat on the love seat.

I stood at the doorway, even though the shotgun was no longer in sight. I had no idea where he'd stashed it, but I didn't trust him.

Or any of them.

"Why were you going to shoot him?" Charity glared at Richard. "How could you?"

Richard sighed, suddenly looking very tired. "Charity, I'm just doing what I've always done. Protecting you. And it's been a job and a half, I'll tell you that." Richard turned to Kyle. "Why are you here?"

Kyle pulled out the newspaper he had shown me and laid it on the table. Ms. Valentine's jaw tightened as Charity looked back and forth in confusion between them.

"What is it?" Charity whispered to Kyle.

"It's an article about the skeleton that was found here," Kyle answered, his jaw tightening.

"Here, as in this house?" Charity asked in her little girl voice.

Kyle nodded.

Charity turned to me, her eyes wide. "It was real?"

"Yes, it was."

Ms. Valentine knocked her knuckles against the side table. "We need to have a discussion, but I think it best that Charity isn't here. Sister, why don't you take a long bath and get cleaned up for dinner tonight? You can put on one of your new dresses."

Charity pouted, but got up and left the room. I watched her leave and noted again how Charity was treated like a child.

"She has a right to know..." Kyle started.

"Not yet." Ms. Valentine cut him off. "You weren't here. You don't know how she took things."

"Things she wouldn't have had to deal with if you all hadn't sent Brian and I away."

"How dare you come back to this house! You betrayed papa! He should have never taken you in," Ms. Valentine hissed. Her hand trembled. She reached for her cane as if needing something to hold. Her eyes flamed as she stared him down.

Kyle ducked his head, shamefaced.

I wanted to speak up, ask so many questions that burned inside me, but I was afraid to remind them I was still there.

Ms. Valentine turned to me. "Charity has the mind of a child, and with Kyle, she's always been like a love-stricken teenager. He got her pregnant and dumped her." Ms. Valentine dabbed at her eyes with a handkerchief. "This is why we tried to protect her. When he panicked and ran, she tried to kill herself. I have given up my life to take care of her."

"Why would she do that?" Kyle asked, looking horrified. "And what could I do? I was in Korea?"

"Because my sister couldn't deal with the pregnancy. She didn't understand that you weren't coming back to marry her!"

"I was married to Marla," Kyle said humbling. "It was a horrible one-night stand, one I barely remember, to be honest. The alcohol..."

"Please. As soon as Marla found out, she divorced you. You were never going to marry Charity. You know it's true. Charity couldn't take care of the baby when he arrived. She didn't want him. Momma tried, and then she died." Ms. Valentine gasped in grief. My eyes darted to the direction Charity had left in, hoping she didn't hear this.

"And when Momma died, it was better for everyone to have you take the baby. We were nearly ruined because of what you and Charity had done. It was better for any part of your poisonous presence to leave our house once and for all, and to *never* return!" Her palm slapped the table. "Yet, here you are."

"I know I wasn't a good man." Kyle shook his head. "But I didn't mean for any of that to happen. Charity and I were never more than friends. It was the night before Richard and I were shipped off. You remember that big going-away party? Well, I got too drunk. Marla and I were fighting. Charity always had a little crush on me. Remember how she carved that heart with our initials on it? Well, that night I made a drunken mistake. One that I paid for with having Marla divorce me while I was overseas. I came back and tried to raise the child as best as I could. Alone."

We sat in a stalemate of bitterness and grief.

"Well, I took care of the problem," Richard said, startling me. He'd been so quiet I'd forgotten he was there.

No one moved. The unsaid meaning of his words roared through the room like ocean sounds hidden in a seashell.

Finally, Ms. Valentine spoke. Her voice cracked. "What do you mean, Richard?"

"I overheard that phone call. The one Kyle made to you all those years ago. I went and picked the boy up. The brat."

"Why would you bring him here?" Ms. Valentine asked. Her eyes widened and she clutched at her throat.

"He had some jewelry that looked worth a lot of money. He said he'd give me more if I'd help him." He wiped down the front of his face with his huge palm. "I figured I could squeeze him a bit and he'd help pay back all he took."

"But instead—" Ms. Valentine prompted.

"Instead he started acting like a loon. Said he needed his fix and was making a huge ruckus." Richard shrugged. "I smothered him with the pillow. End of story."

I grabbed the door frame, reeling with horror. Kyle cried out, and even Ms. Valentine looked green.

"He was a product of sin. You live a life of filth, you die by the sword." Richard glared at us, daring us to argue.

It was then I remembered the Bible scripture that had been highlighted by the picture of the baby. It had been Richard who'd done that.

Kyle began to cry, clutching his forehead as he leaned over. "It should have been me!"

"Yes, it should have." Ms. Valentine responded, her voice cold. She had regained her composure.

There was a knock on the door.

I'd forgotten that the police were on their way.

The knock quickly turned into pounding. Ms. Valentine rose to answer it. She grabbed my shoulder on her way out. "Nothing good can come from the police's involvement. What's done is done. We're going to agree that Richard thought there was an intruder, but it turned out to be a family friend who hadn't gotten a response at the front door and was trying the back. Richard was just a startled old man trying to protect his sisters."

I watched her go, my mind spinning. I felt bad about the two sisters being left alone. But my mind was made up. Richard had to be held responsible for his actions, something I didn't think the Valentines had much experience with.

Ms. Valentine met the cops at the door. One of the cops was Officer Carlson. He was the same one who had come to my house, accusing me of being a bit "Hollywood" with my drama. He walked in and narrowed his eyes when he saw me. It was enough to tell me he was thinking he had been spot on with his assessment.

"Ms. O'Neil," he said, with a nod. "We meet again."

CHAPTER 23

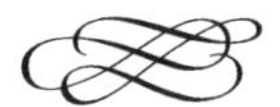

It was a rough next two hours. Charity cried with confusion. Ms. Valentine threatened everyone, thumping her cane and yelling, "This is outrageous!" One of the officers forced her to sit and cautioned her that the cane was about to be taken away.

Speaking of taking away, that's exactly what they did to Richard. They turned him around to cuff him when his gaze landed on me. "I should have ran you off the road that night! I knew you were a no-good snoop!"

"Quiet," warned the officer who was cuffing him.

I shivered and turned to face Officer Carlson. He'd been recording my statement, which really seemed to be asking the same questions over and over. He was so tall, my neck was starting to ache looking up at him.

He raised an eyebrow. "At least we know now who was chasing you. You are quite the case solver. That's three in one day."

"Three?" I asked. I staggered back a bit. I was feeling dizzy from all the adrenaline rushes. I needed a burger STAT.

He reached out a hand to steady me. "You okay?"

I nodded.

His gaze was filled with concern. Finally, he seemed to believe I wasn't about to tip over and removed his hand. Talking to me like I was a toddler, he lifted a finger. "One, the mystery guy was chasing you. Two, who the skeleton was. And three, who shot Officer Benson after the jewelry store robbery."

I glanced at Kyle. my cheeks hot with fear. It had been Kyle's first time hearing what his son had done that day, all those years ago. He sat on the couch with his head in his hands, obviously devastated.

Officer Carlson went over the story one more time. I had to resist rolling my eyes in impatience. Finally, he held something out for me to sign.

I scribbled my name on it and handed back the pen.

"Okay, Miss O'Neil. You are free to go," he said, after taking the paper from me. "You planning on staying in town?"

"Yeah."

He didn't say anything more, just moved to where his buddy stood taking pictures. I wondered why he asked. Was it because he might have more questions?

Kyle saw the cop leave and slowly stood up and walked over.

"How you doing?" he asked.

"Kind of exhausted. How about you?"

"Mutual. You heading out now?"

I nodded.

"Let me walk you to your car."

I was vaguely relieved that he offered to walk me out. Now that things had settled down, I still had another burning question.

"When did you leave Morocco?" I asked. His eyebrows rumpled together and he frowned, confused. I hurried to clarify. "Gaila Crawford. She mentioned you sent her something from Morocco."

"Oh." He nodded with a sad smile. "Years ago, I was a roadie with this Indie group. They played sort of middle eastern music and had exotic animals and things like that. I still keep in touch with a few of them. I sent one of my friends a letter to send her from there." His sheepish response wasn't answer enough.

"Why did you do that?" Then I flushed, realizing how rude that sounded. "I know it's none of my business. But I can't help but be curious. I've been up to my eyebrows in everyone's history. Besides, she's such a nice lady."

"Yeah. You're right, she is. So, it will probably come as no surprise to you that I had a thing for her years ago. We actually became friends after she married. I tried to be respectful of that, but still liked to keep in touch here and there."

That reminded me of something. I reached into my pants where I'd stashed my new good luck charm. I glanced at it, wondering what reaction it was going to evoke out of Kyle. Slowly, I held my hand out.

He studied it for a second before a slow smile crawled across his face. "No way!" He reached out and took the squirrel. "Charity gave me this when I first started hanging out with Richard. Where did you get it?"

"From Mrs. Crawford. She told me it was a good luck charm that you'd given her years ago." I chuckled. "She figured I might need it dealing with the Valentines."

His thumb rubbed over the figurine. "I guess it brought you luck, then."

I shrugged. I mean, I was still alive and the mystery solved. So I guessed it could be true.

His eyes had a dreamy look as he stared at the squirrel. "Charity used to get those all the time. They came in a tea box. My luck was never that great after I gave it away. Maybe I should have kept it."

"You can have it back," I said.

"Really? I mean, if Gaila...."

"Please! Keep it. I'm sure she'd want you to have it, too."

He smiled. "Thank you. That means a lot."

We'd arrived at my car by now. I reached for the handle and then hesitated. "You sure you're okay? How was it to see Charity again?" I asked.

"Sad." He stared at the house. "I wanted to talk to her about Brian, but she's not... it seems like she never grew up. We'd never been more than friends, except for that one drunken night. But we had a son together. I thought she'd care about him, but it's like she's forgotten she ever had him or something. Maybe if she'd stayed in his life, things would have turned out differently. I don't know."

Awkwardly, I patted his arm. After all he'd been through, I really wanted closure for him. It might come, but I could tell it wasn't going to look like he expected. "I'm sorry."

He rubbed his neck, dark with a tan. "Life, man."

"Confusing at the best of times," I filled in. "Not to mention, people make their own choices. No matter how much we want them to make the right one, it's still up to them."

He nodded and slipped the figurine into his pocket.

As he did it, I asked, "What about Mrs. Crawford? She might like to hear from you."

"You think?"

"Sure."

His brow crinkled, and his eyes softened. "I might stop to say hi on my way out."

"I think that would be a good thing." I didn't quite know how to say goodbye. I reached out and touched his arm. "I am sorry about Brian."

He nodded. "It was a long time ago, but it will always haunt me. As will this house."

His words tugged at my heart. "Take care of yourself."

We said goodbye and I got in my car. I watched him in the

mirror as he returned to the house, maybe to say his final goodbyes to Charity.

It was with a very introspective heart that I backed out of the driveway and drove home. Life was so strange, and wild, and unbelievably full of confusion, love, and beauty. It's no wonder we, as humans, tried to box up our emotions to stay safe. It took a ton of courage to open up to all the craziness.

The sun stretched long golden fingers over the now-tilled fields. I flipped on the heat and bit at a hangnail.

Deep thoughts haunted me. Who was I in all of this mess?

I thought about everything that happened at the house. How I'd stood between a man and a gun. How I'd heard a father cry in regret.

I knew one thing. I wanted to be braver. I wanted to be known as a person courageous enough to be open to change. I wanted to live out my hopes without regret.

I thought of my great-great grandma. How she'd hidden away in hay stacks to escape from Hitler. How she'd taken refuge on a boat and petitioned for a new life in a country where she knew no one.

Courage.

My dad had said to remember that her blood ran through my

veins. I nodded, making my decision. Ten minutes later, I flipped on the blinker and turned onto Baker Street.

The road was dirt and short. Too short, today. Tall trees that I still wasn't sure of their names grew along the sides. Their sweeping branches touched overhead.

His driveway was to the left. My face flushed with nerves, but I didn't chicken out. Not this time. I turned down it and parked.

The house was a white two-story. A pair of rocking chairs sat on the porch next to a small table.

I stood there in the dirt driveway and studied it for a moment. What it would have felt like had I done this sooner. Maybe even with my father as a little girl. Would I have come here for Christmas? Birthdays? Or would the door had always remained closed.

Would it remain locked tight now?

My heart hammered. I swallowed hard.

You can do this. You have the blood of a warrior woman in your veins.

Brave words, but my legs shook as I slowly stepped forward. I forced myself. I wasn't going to back down now.

I knocked on the door. Through the dirty window, I spotted a fluffy rocket race, barking, down the hallway. A second later, a gruff voice yelled out, "Bear! Come back here! Confound it!"

My breath caught in my throat at the sight of a short man, with hair bristling out like cotton candy, appeared around the corner. He came down the hall after the dog, yelling up a storm. Perched on his nose were thick glasses. Plaid slippers scuffed against the wooden floor.

He opened the door with a scowl. My mouth felt dryer than a sawdust pile.

"Help you?" he asked, his voice sounding like he'd gargled gravel. His eyes narrowed behind the glasses as he studied me.

"Oscar O'Neil?" I started. My hands trembled, and I squeezed them together.

"Yes." And then to the little Pomeranian hopping at his feet, he yelled, "Bear, stop it. Get down. Blast it! Peanut! Be good!"

As soon as he yelled out the name Peanut, the dog sat. Her butt wiggled on the floor and I saw that, even while sitting, her tail wagged. I smiled, and then looked back at the man.

"I'm Stella." My voice caught in my throat, and I choked out, "Stella O'Neil."

He stared at me for a moment as the words tumbled through his brain. Then his mouth dropped. "Stella?"

I nodded.

"My boy Steve's little girl?"

I nodded again. A lump was in my throat. I didn't think I could say any more.

He threw open his arms, throwing out the scent of cigars and Old Spice. "Come here. Let me—" He didn't finish his request. I saw his eyes puddling up behind his glasses. Immediately, I fell into his arms.

He hugged me tight, and then I felt his chest heave. "Stella. I have missed you so much. Welcome home."

I was teary myself ,and my heart melted at the warm reception. I could never have imagined what this seemingly innocuous moment had in store in the future for me.

But I was about to find out.

The End

UNTITLED

Thank you for reading Mind your Manors. There's more! Be sure to catch Stella's new adventure in—

A Dead Market

Home Strange Home

Duplex Double Trouble

MidCentury Modern Murder

With Killer Views

Here are a few more series to whet your appetite.

Baker Street Mysteries— join Georgie, amateur sleuth and historical tour guide on her spooky, crazy adventures. As a fun bonus there's free recipes included!

Cherry Pie or Die

Cookies and Scream

Crème Brûlée or Slay

Drizzle of Death

Slash in the Pan

Oceanside Hotel Cozy Mysteries—Maisie runs a 5 star hotel and thought she'd seen everything. Little did she know. From haunted pirate tales to Hollywood red carpet events, she has a lot to keep her busy.

Booked For Murder

Deadly Reservation

Final Check Out

Fatal Vacancy

Suite Casualty

Angel Lake Cozy Mysteries—Elise comes home to her home town to lick her wounds after a nasty divorce. Together, with her best friend Lavina, they cook up some crazy mysteries.

The Sweet Taste of Murder

The Bitter Taste of Betrayal

The Sour Taste of Suspicion

The Honeyed Taste of Deception

The Tempting Taste of Danger

The Frosty Taste of Scandal

And here is Circus Cozy Mysteries— Meet Trixie, the World's Smallest Lady Godiva. She may be small but she's learning she has a lion's heart.

Cirque de Slay

Big Top Treachery

Made in the USA
Coppell, TX
07 March 2020

16597219R00132